Loving a Billionaire

By

Marie Higgins

ONE

Police Detective Talia Russell, from Honolulu, Hawaii's precinct, raised her fist to knock on the door, but as she rapped on the hardwood, the barrier pushed open. She held her breath and listened for signs of movement inside the penthouse apartment.

Holding her breath, she peeked around the edge of the door, hoping to see someone standing there. Nothing but air greeted her.

She frowned. Why had the door just opened when her informant assured her that the CEO of the Imperial Hawaiian's Grand Hotel, Austin Reeder, would be in a meeting all day? Apparently, her informant wasn't very accurate.

She cleared her throat and called into the quiet apartment, "This is Detective Russell with Honolulu's Task Force. I need to ask you a few questions."

Still, she heard nothing.

Talia opened her decorative, black, beaded purse that hung over her shoulder, and grabbed her cell phone, quickly dialing her partner. *Hamill here. I'm busy, so leave a message.*

She growled. Where was he? He was supposed to be here with her. "Kurt, get your butt over here, pronto. I'm at Austin Reeder's suite, and I think there might be a break-in… or maybe even another murder scene. The door is cracked open, but I don't hear anything inside. So get over here—" *click*. The phone disconnected and she grumbled under her breath.

"Mr. Reeder?" she called into the room. "Are you there? Are you hurt?"

Once again, she heard nothing but silence.

Glancing at the elevator, she tried to decide what to do. She couldn't go inside the suite until Kurt showed up. It was too dangerous to go in alone. But because her partner wasn't answering his phone…

A heavy thud came from inside the penthouse suite. Her heart knocked against her ribs harder, and she quickly grasped her Glock inside her purse. She still didn't dare go inside. She was overdressed for this particular assignment, but when Sergeant James Feakes told her to check out one of the suspects – insisting it was to be done now – who was Talia to argue? Besides, when the sergeant wanted something immediately, he didn't want to hear excuses. Trying to explain that Talia was at her father's, and soon-to-be stepmother's, afternoon engagement party wouldn't have hit the stubborn sergeant's ears, anyway.

Her red and white floral print, off-the-shoulders short-sleeved Polynesian dress that hugged her figure and showed off too much of her legs, was definitely not the required uniform. Unfortunately, she was here to do her job, no matter what she looked like. However, the other police officers she worked with would get a hearty chuckle over this, which meant they could *never* find out.

Another heavy thud came from inside. "Mr. Reeder? Can you hear me?"

When she didn't hear him, instinct told her that she needed to go inside and check it out. Taking careful steps, she entered the room with her G42 weapon held high. Along with the gun, she quickly swept her gaze around the room, but so far, it appeared the occupant wasn't in residence.

She wasn't surprised to see Mr. Reeder's place decorated with expensive chairs, antique furniture, and Persian rugs. The man was extremely rich. She wouldn't be surprised if he owned his own airplane. He also owned the chain of luxury hotels in Hawaii and all over the United States.

As she took three more steps, her three-inch heels tapped on the tiled floor of the entryway. Silently, she groaned. This was one of the reasons she'd wanted to go home and change, but Sergeant Feakes wouldn't have it.

"Is anyone here?" she called out again but received no reply.

Although she really should turn and leave, her gut feeling told her to stay. She had heard heavy thuds. If Mr. Reeder wasn't here, perhaps this was a break-in after all. That would certainly explain why the front door was cracked open.

4

Talia should search his penthouse suite. He was a suspect of a murder, after all.

The victim of the brutal murder was twenty-six year old, Kalama Kane. The woman had been a religious girl in high school, but once she graduated and went to college, she spent her time at bars and single's clubs.

Kalama had been murdered in her family's home right here in Honolulu. Her parents were at work, and her younger brother was at school. Kalama had just gotten out of the tub and wrapped a robe around her body. Within moments of leaving the bathroom, the woman was smashed over the head with a large object, crushing her skull, and killing her instantly.

Suspiciously, the murder weapon wasn't found on the premises. No fingerprints were anywhere on the crime scene, except for the family who lived there. The only thing the police had to use for leads was the list of men written on a piece of paper that was folded and placed in Kalama's robe.

Since that discovery, Talia's task force team had been trying to locate the men on the list and interview them. Austin Reeder's name was at the bottom of the list. Talia and her partner, Kurt Hamill, had planned to visit Mr. Reeder tomorrow for questioning.

Why Sergeant Feakes wanted this done immediately, Talia wished she knew. And where was Kurt? As her partner, he should have been here to back her up.

She reached into her beaded purse again, pulled out her cell, and texted her partner. *Where are you? I know you received Feakes' call. Why are you ignoring me?*

As she slid the cell back in her purse, she seriously hoped he was on the way. Backup was most important in her line of work.

A bead of moisture trickled down her neck. Good grief! Why did it feel overly warm in here? It was early summer, so why did it feel like it was hotter than ninety-five degrees?

She clutched her G42 and walked into the room further. The wealthy businessman had a glass-case liquor bar, a large dining area, and living room. The three bookcases filled from edge to edge. It would seem he didn't have a social life, and probably stayed at home reading. She'd had almost this many books when she was in college, and of course, she really didn't have a social life, either.

Talia took another step, heading toward the hallway, but before reaching it, the floor creaked. She jerked to a stop and listened closer.

The door to one of the rooms opened, and out walked a man. He was tall, built like a quarterback, and wore a black bathrobe that reached below his knees. His wet hair was slicked back on his head, and his face appeared freshly shaven. His attention was on his iPhone as he scrolled through it. In his ears were earphones with a cord attached to the electronic device.

Inwardly, she groaned. No wonder he hadn't heard her calling out, announcing herself. *A good detective checks every room, Russell.* But in her defense, she was about to when he walked out.

Panic hammered away in her chest, bringing a momentary shut-down to her brain... and her lungs, because at this moment as she stared at his bathrobe and the muscular bare legs, she couldn't breathe. Her worst nightmare had come true. She'd been caught in the suspect's penthouse apartment looking like a girl going to her first prom, and holding a G42, no less! What kind of bad horror flick was this?

The rhythm of her heart was as fast as a motorboat zooming over the high waves during a typhoon, and she knew her heart would crash and sink at any moment. If that happened, she'd be standing in the middle of his room, looking like a complete idiot in a fancy dress, with a gun.

What would he think when he saw her? Although she could imagine plenty, it worried her that she didn't look like a police detective. Naturally, he'd think someone was here to end his life. She definitely didn't want him thinking that.

Without another thought, she pushed the Glock back in her beaded purse. Within seconds, the man raised his head and looked at her. He stopped. His mouth hung open as his gaze moved over her. It didn't bother her the way he scanned up and down her body like some kind of hungry jaguar, but what concerned her was the way her mouth dried so quickly and cotton had taken up residence in her throat. This man was absolutely the most handsome man she'd ever laid eyes on – and she'd seen many in her twenty-five years.

Talia forced herself to breathe… in through the nose, out of the mouth… before the oxygen stopped transporting to her brain. This handsome man made it impossible to concentrate. From his wet, short dark hair, to the cotton robe wrapped around his muscular frame, giving her a peep-show of his bare legs, was it any wonder her mind was so mixed up?

Willing the words to come to her mind, she struggled with an excuse of what to tell him as to why she was in his apartment. Standing before him without her Glock made her feel naked, and of course, brain dead. She certainly wasn't being professional now. *Sergeant Feakes is going to ask for my badge and gun!*

Mr. Reeder's narrowed gaze stayed on her as he walked toward her, pulling out his earphones. When he finally stopped in front of her, the suspicious glint to his eyes had disappeared. A sexy, crooked grin touched his mouth.

Sexy? She tried to shake the image out of her head. He was a murder suspect! Thinking of him this way was against the rules, and she kept the police force's rulebook in her head at all times.

"Aloha," he said, warily.

"Al –" her voice cracked, so she cleared it and started over. "Aloha."

"How did you get in?" he asked.

"I… um," she swallowed hard, "the door was already opened a little. I… heard a heavy thump inside. I… didn't know what to think except you had fallen or something."

He nodded. "Oh, that. Well, I accidentally knocked the hamper over." He ran his gaze over her again. "So I suppose you decided to come today, anyway?"

The deep timbre in his voice made her heart flip-flop. Yet, why had he asked that question? What did he mean? Perhaps he knew who she was and wondered why she was here today instead of tomorrow. But how could he know her purpose for being here? Especially dressed like this?

She clutched her hands and held them to her middle. If only she had her fingers wrapped around the handle of her gun, she'd feel more secure. She grumbled under her breath. What was she thinking to put it away so soon?

"You don't need to be afraid of me," he spoke again. "In fact, why don't you come over here?" He motioned to the dinette table. He slid his iPhone into the pocket of his robe. "We'll have a drink to break the awkwardness between us."

Slowly, she shook her head. He had no clue to her identity. Nobody asked a police detective to have a drink of liquor with them. Maybe a cup of coffee or a soda, but never liquor.

Now the question remained, who then, did he think she was? For some reason, Mr. Reeder wasn't at all surprised to see a strange woman who dressed this fancy in his apartment in the middle of the day. And yet, he wasn't dressed like he was going out for a night on the town, as she was.

Perhaps she should play along and see where it led. After all, she was a detective, and she'd do anything to get the answers to her questions. Well, almost anything.

TWO

Trying to relax her stiff legs, Talia wobbled to the table that was fancy enough for royalty to sit at. The Victorian style set came with matching mahogany, cushioned chairs. Hesitantly, she sat on one of the chairs. She didn't take her eyes off him when he walked to the liquor cabinet, reached into the glass cabinet and took out two glasses.

"What would you like to drink?" he asked. "I have just about everything there is."

She couldn't stop gaping at his magnificent build. Her brain told her to stop, because she loathed it when others looked upon her as if she was dessert served on an ancient Polynesian platter with a golden spoon. But how could she stop admiring something so magnificent? Even the way he moved was sensual, like a model that'd been trained to turn a woman's head.

He glanced at her over his shoulder as if waiting for an answer. She licked her dry lips. She wasn't a big drinker, even at special occasions when it called for champagne, she was usually the one turning it down and asking for ice water with a lemon. And because she was on duty, drinking was definitely out of the question.

Mr. Reeder's eyes narrowed on her again. His intent stare brought her out of her thoughts, and yet, her mind still remained blank. Silently, she scolded herself for acting this way. He wasn't that good-looking, was he? *Oh, yes, he is!* But she still needed to quit acting like a deaf mute.

She cleared her throat, preparing to say something, even if it was stupid. This had to be the longest she'd gone without speaking.

"I'm assuming Ariki sent you." He grinned and his eyes twinkled.

Are his eyes green? That wouldn't be a good thing. She'd not met many men with green eyes here on the island, but green had always been her favorite color. And of course, Mr. Reeder's were very dreamy.

Her mind quickly came out of the clouds and consumed his question. Who was Ariki? Well, since she was already in character – whatever character he thought she was – she'd play along. She nodded instead of verbally replying. Where was her voice?

His smile widened. "Please don't be scared. Loosen up a little. I'm going to have brandy, would you like one?"

She shouldn't, but... She didn't have to drink it. Instead, she'd just act like it. That would be good enough. She gave him another nod.

His long, lean fingers plucked off the bottle cork of the crystal decanter and poured the rich amber colored liquid into two crystal goblets. He brought the drinks to the table and rested one on a coaster in front of her.

"I'm not used to talking to myself." He chuckled lightly. "Can you at least tell me your name?"

She swallowed, moistening the cotton dryness in her mouth. "Tali—" she squeaked.

His dark eyebrows drew together. "Your name is Talley?"

She cleared her throat. *Russell, what is wrong with you?* "No, it's Talia."

When his expression relaxed, relief poured over her. His sensual grin returned and made her body weak. She silently cursed the effect. Perhaps it was the heat in the room. Why else would her brain refuse to work? She was a police detective, not a simpering female who swooned at the first smile from a good-looking man.

"You have such a pretty name. It's almost angelic. It makes me wonder if you're really an angel from Heaven sent here to put me on the straight and narrow."

She bit her tongue to keep from snickering. That was a line she'd heard before. All through the two years of college, and then at the Police Academy, she'd been propositioned one way or another and heard almost all the pick-up lines in the book. She'd ignored the sleazy men her father had warned her about and concentrated on her studies. But this particular pick-up line took her by surprise, mainly because she didn't expect a man of his caliber to actually use it on a woman.

"So, my shy Talia," Mr. Reeder's voice took on a hint of humor, "what can I do for the petite and delicately beautiful woman sitting at my table?"

Once again, his compliment took her off guard. Against her will, her heart pounded faster. With a shaky hand, she lifted the drink to her lips and pretended to sip. She noticed his gaze wandered over her dress again, and then to her legs. Why was he so bold with his inspection? She didn't think she'd spilled food on her dress during the brief time she was at her father's and soon-to-be stepmother's engagement social.

"So you're one of Ariki's friends." He took a quick drink of his brandy, his gaze never leaving her eyes. "Tell me, Talia, how long have you known Ariki?"

Talia should be drilling him with questions, but since he thought she was someone else, playing along was essential. She'd already led him to believe she was new, so she quickly thought up an answer. "About two weeks."

He took another sip of his drink. "Ariki can sure be funny at times, don't you think?"

"Why do you say that?"

"He told me he was fixing me up with a girl he'd just met, but he didn't tell me how gorgeous you are." He winked.

Her face heated quickly, and she inwardly cursed her body's reaction. Good grief! She had never acted this way before. It must be the heat in the room, for sure. There was no other explanation for it.

What was it about his compliments that made her feel like a girl experiencing her first school crush? Many men had tried to dish out compliments, and she usually tossed their comments aside, knowing they were just words without meaning.

"So, what's your specialty?" he asked.

She inhaled sharply. What was he talking about?

"You know," he continued, sitting in the chair across from her, "Ariki wouldn't have fixed us up if he didn't think we would have a good time tonight."

She about choked on her own saliva. "A… good time?"

He laughed deeply. "Yes. Isn't that why you're here? To entertain me?"

Talia's mind swirled with confusion. He couldn't possibly mean *that*. Yet, what else could he mean? Did he think she was a call girl or something? That would be the biggest insult of all.

Irritation flowed through her and she bit her lip. She couldn't ruin her cover now. She hadn't gotten any answers about the murder, so she had to keep pretending. Of course, now she needed to figure out some kind of specialty just to keep their conversation going so that she could learn more. "Well, I give a really good mind-blowing massage."

He continued to grin at her in his devilish way. She was sure he'd charmed many women just by smiling at them. She liked the way the corners of his perfect mouth lifted, because it made her heart thud a little quicker. The feeling wasn't totally uncomfortable. In fact, it was almost relaxing.

She didn't consider herself pretty in any way, but she'd had the kind of toned body the guys in college liked – physical enough to take them on at anything. Growing up with three brothers kept her in shape, and she competed with them in most sports. However, she knew even in high school, that if a guy didn't like her for her mind, he wasn't worth it.

Mr. Reeder would be the type of man who went out with a woman just because her beauty matched his. Then again, Talia was sure he'd be able to get any woman he wanted. All he had to do was smile.

Trying to shake away the burning interest in this man that grew inside of her like Jack's magic beans in his fairy-tale story, she decided it was time to take control of the situation. How else would she discover if he had anything to do with Kalama Kane's murder?

She tilted back the goblet of brandy to her mouth, and pretended to drink again. After placing it back on the coaster, she rose from the chair and walked toward him. She motioned to the chair for him to sit.

He followed her direction and sat. Hesitantly, she placed her fingers on the muscular cords of his neck, just inside his bathrobe. Warm sensations shot through her, and she bit her lip from groaning aloud. Her fingers nearly melted against his smooth skin. *This is going to be harder than I thought.*

Come on, Russell, you're a cop, so start acting like one!

Dropping his shoulders, he tilted his head forward. "Umm... your fingers are magical."

Encouraged, she smiled and rubbed his neck gently, experiencing that feeling of control she'd always enjoyed while giving massages. The clean spicy, manly scent of his body shot strange signals to her brain, and her own tension began to unwind.

She needed to start drilling him for answers. "So, Austin. Can I call you Austin?"

"Yes. I like the way it sounds when you say it."

He was such a flirt. "So, Austin, how long have you known Ariki?"

When she pushed her fingers a little harder into his neck muscles, a deep moan escaped his throat. Against her will, shivers of delight skipped across her skin as warmth spread through her middle. *Stop this insanity, Russell. He's just a normal man...who happens to be built like Adonis and is the most handsome man I've ever laid my eyes on.*

"Ariki was the first man I hired to work for me when I had this hotel built, and we've stayed friends. Of course, he's no longer in the hotel business."

She needed to know more. "I wonder why he wanted to set us up."

"Because Ariki knows I don't have time for a real relationship." Austin chuckled. "How pathetic is it that I don't even have time to find my own dates?"

"Has he set you up with other women?"

"Yes."

"If you don't mind me asking, who was the last girl?"

"Kalama." His voice was lower. "But since I'd known her from my past, we were just friends. It's too bad what happened to her. It's hard to believe someone I was friends with was brutally murdered."

Talia's spirits lifted. Finally, the topic she wanted to discuss. Was it a coincidence? She'd figure that out later. Right now, she'd ask him more questions.

"Yes, Kalama's murder came as a complete shock to all of us. It makes me wonder why anyone would want to kill her."

"I don't know," he mumbled, sleepily.

"Did you like her?" she probed.

"Oh, she was nice enough, I guess. But more often than not, she nagged me. I just don't have tolerance for women like that," he said in softer tones.

Talia gritted her teeth. That wasn't telling her anything. Not really. She really wanted to know if he was involved with Kalama right before she died. In Kalama's small bungalow where she'd called home near the beach, Talia had noticed the woman owned several pieces of expensive jewelry, and she owned three closets full of fancy clothes. Yet, the girl had only worked part-time as a secretary at one of the resorts. Talia and Kurt suspected Kalama was some rich man's mistress.

Talia blinked with wide eyes as the puzzle pieces began fitting together. What were the odds she'd found Kalama's killer already? After all, Mr. Reeder was a rich man. He'd dated Kalama before she died. Talia wondered if this Ariki guy had something to do with the murder, too. Was it some kind of love-triangle?

She dared not ask, but it was her duty as a detective to find out the truth. Part of her didn't want to think a handsome, sweet-talking man like Mr. Reeder could be a cold-blooded killer. There was only one way to find out, and she must be blunt about it.

"Austin? Were... um, were you and Kalama involved with each other?"

THREE

Austin Reeder was thoroughly exhausted since he hadn't rested for forty-eight hours, and he should have told Talia to come back another day. But after feeling her healing fingers massaging his neck, he realized he'd made the right decision to keep her here. Her touch awakened more than just the stiff muscles of his neck. Now, he couldn't wait to get to know her a little better. His friend had done well in finding this woman for Austin.

Her question, however, made him chuckle. He took hold of Talia's soft hand and pulled it around his neck and to his mouth. He pressed a kiss on her wrist. She was confusing him, which wasn't too hard to do because he was extremely tired today. But what was her game? Why had she acted so innocent? And especially, why was she asking such personal questions? Most of the girls that Ariki had set up with Austin knew not to ask about his life. There were just some things that people didn't need to know, especially women who were just one-night-stands, or possibly *two*-nights.

Maybe he should send Talia home after all. Ariki's so-called birthday surprise wasn't appreciated right now. Not when Austin couldn't make this meeting useful because he was a walking zombie. He'd told Ariki not to send him anyone for his birthday, but his friend had never listened before, so why should he start now? Ariki also enjoyed clowning around. Was this one of his friend's jokes?

"You have such wonderful hands, Talia."

"Mahalo," she thanked him in a tight voice, using her homeland's language, as she pulled her hand away.

Right now in his exhausted state, he wanted her hands back on his neck so he could feel the warmth flowing through his body from her tender touch. But apparently, she wanted to talk. Strange, since most of the girls Ariki found for him rarely wanted to talk.

Sighing, he relaxed back in the chair. Thankfully, she returned to massaging his neck. "You think Kalama and I were involved with each other? Do you mean like lovers?" He laughed weakly. "How could we be lovers if there was no love between us?"

"Really? Did you have any feelings for her?"

"Nothing more than just friends." He paused as his mind clouded with doubts. "Talia, why are you asking these questions? What does it have to do with your time with me?"

Her fingers froze, as did the hot breath blowing against his neck. Suddenly, she stepped back.

"I guess it's time for me to go," she whispered.

His breath stalled in his throat. He couldn't let her leave now, especially since her actions made him confused, and he hated feeling confused.

When she tried to move past him, he grabbed hold of her arm. "Hey, Talia, I'm truly sorry about today. I'm extremely exhausted, and I must apologize. I've been up for forty-eight hours straight making a business deal."

The smile she gave him was fake as her gaze bounced between his eyes and the grip he had on her arm. "That's all right. I understand."

He didn't want her to leave like this. Ariki would be upset at Austin for brushing her off so easily. Austin pulled on her arm and her legs bumped against his exposed knees, making his robe part, displaying part of his knee. Her gaze fell to his knee and her eyes widened. He nearly laughed. What was with her innocent act?

"Talia, since I don't want you to think that coming here was a total waste of your time, will you do something for me?"

Slowly her gaze lifted and met his eyes. "What's that?"

"Will you give me a kiss?"

Confusion consumed her expression along with the crimson color spreading to her beautiful Polynesian cheeks. Once again, he wanted to laugh. She acted like an innocent girl, fresh out of an all girl's school. That's probably what Ariki had done – found him a girl who was soon going to become a nun.

When he first saw Talia standing in his living room, she looked like most of the girls Ariki had fixed up for him; sexy dress, with long hair flowing over their shoulders. Talia was no different, except she was a lot prettier and her hair was wound in a bun. He really liked how toned her body was, but he especially liked her shiny black hair. Touching it to see if it was as silky as it appeared was tempting, but he really was tired and needed sleep. However, he could spare a few minutes for her kiss. It would give him something to dream about.

"I... don't think so, Austin. Not this time. As you said, you're really tired, and I should be going."

This one was a tease. Ariki must have paid her good money to trick Austin. Well, he couldn't have that. He'd show his friend who was in charge now.

Playfully, he tugged on her arm, pulling her nearer. "Come on, sweetie. I don't want you leaving here thinking you haven't earned your payment."

Suddenly, her bright red face faded, leaving it almost white. Panic coated her wide eyes. Even her lips quivered.

She licked her lips and gave him a shaky smile. "Well, if you insist. Now let me go."

The fear in her eyes worried him. So perhaps he'd been mistaken about Ariki's joke. Obviously, this woman was nervous. Either that or she was a very good actress.

Her chest rose and fell quickly, and the gushes of air coming out of her mouth blew across his face. He should stop this immediately. He'd never been one to force a woman, and he wasn't going to start now.

Her legs shook as she stepped toward him. He held up a hand to stop her. "Talia, I'm not going to make you do anything if you don't want to—"

Suddenly, she fell against him. Whether she'd tripped, or if falling was done on purpose, she landed halfway across his lap. Her face flamed a deeper red as the palms of her hands moved over his chest. One slipped inside of his robe to his neck, and he sucked in a breath. The touch was electrifying and jolted him alert.

Her eyes widened. Up this close he could see the color was brown, a very lovely brown. Almost a rust color, in fact. Her skin was lighter than most of the Polynesian people on this island.

Mumbling her apologies, she tried to stand, but all she could manage was to fall on his lap again. The embarrassment was evident on her bright face. He felt sorry for her, and he should try to make her relax so the awkward moment would pass quickly.

"It's all right, Talia." He stroked her soft bare arms. "I'm not going to hurt you. Take a deep breath and try to calm yourself."

She closed her eyes and must have given up the idea that he was a scorching stove setting her on fire, because within seconds, her body relaxed, and she sat sideways on his lap. He continued to rub up and down her arms until her ragged breathing sounded mostly normal. Her body still quivered slightly, but she seemed more in control, now.

"Are you feeling better?" he asked.

She opened her eyes and met his stare. "Yes, Austin."

Her voice was so soft, he could hardly hear. It almost sounded as if she sighed his name. When realization finally hit him, his heart leapt. She *had* sighed his name, and it sounded so sweet the way it rolled off her tongue.

Had this innocence of hers been an act? Because now her eyes told him a different story and fear was not a chapter in this tale at all. Her gaze moved slowly over his face, coming to rest on his mouth. Was she going to kiss him? He'd only accept it as long as she didn't think he was forcing her.

"Talia, if you don't want to kiss me, you don't have to."

"I don't?"

"No." He trailed his fingers from her shoulder, up her neck to her face in gentle caresses. "I don't know what Ariki told you about me, but I'm not forceful."

"That's good to know."

He waited for her to scoot off his lap, but she didn't. He also realized one of her hands still rested inside on his chest, and her fingers slowly slid back and forth across the hollow of his throat. He'd been so tired only moments ago, but her caress had brought him wide awake.

"You know, you have a very soft touch," he said.

"So do you."

Her breathing had changed again and became just as ragged as his. One thing was certain… if she didn't make the first move and kiss him, he was going to do it.

He brushed his fingers across her bottom lip and her lips parted. It was now or never.

FOUR

Hesitantly, Austin leaned forward, waiting for her to stop him. But when she met his descending mouth, excitement filled him. As he touched her lips with his, fireworks shot off in his head, and he cupped her face. Another sigh breezed from her throat, but this time he didn't stop to figure out what she had said.

Austin moved his lips back and forth with hers. She clutched his robe, and thankfully, didn't pull away. He slid his hands around to her back and urged her closer. A low moan rattled in her throat, and he turned the kiss wilder.

No longer did he need sleep. He needed this, instead. He needed the crazy beating of his heart as though this was his first time kissing a woman so passionate. He needed to know this woman with the intoxicating kisses desired him as much as he desired her.

The only thing that would make this moment better was to know that she wanted *him*, and not his money. He rarely told women exactly how much he earned per year, only because he wanted to find one who would see past his bank account and like him for himself.

He doubted even Ariki knew Austin was a billionaire.

He moved his hands to her neck, and they knocked against the awkward tilt of the bun in her hair. Without asking permission, he slipped his fingers in her hair and pulled out the pins holding the style together, and dropped the objects to the floor. Her hair cascaded down her back, reaching below her hips, and feeling just as silky as he'd imagined.

Following his example, she threaded her fingers through his hair, still keeping up with his urgent kisses.

"You're absolutely beautiful," he murmured against her mouth. "I could kiss you all night long."

Another low moan came from her, but the sound was different this time. Almost sorrowful. Suddenly, her body stiffened, and she pulled away. Passion was evident on her expression, but so was fear.

"I… I shouldn't have done this," she whispered as she tried to stand.

"No, Talia. Don't stop—"

"I have to."

Her voice was sharp this time, and she jumped to her feet, quickly moving away from him as fast as she could go.

"Talia—" He stood and tried to catch her, but the woman was already sprinting out of the door. "Talia, stop. I can't have you leave me like this."

She threw him a glare for a few seconds before she entered the elevator. The doors closed before he could reach her.

Sighing, he leaned his forehead against the wall. There was something about this woman. She was vastly different from the others Ariki had fixed up for him. And he enjoyed the difference.

As he made his way back into his penthouse suite and closed the door, weariness consumed his body again, reminding him how he hadn't slept for forty-eight hours. Although his body was exhausted, his mind was not.

One way or another, he'd figure out how to find that woman. Next time, he'd make it so she wasn't afraid of him.

* * * *

Talia stared at her reflection in the shiny steel walls of the elevator. Tears pooled in her eyes. Her hair hung down around her shoulders, and her mouth was swollen from his passionate kisses. Inside, she died of shame.

Why had she kissed him? Anger welled up inside of her, mixed with disgust. Why hadn't she remembered that she was a police detective? She was actually a very good detective. But nobody would know it now.

Disgrace rocked through her body, making her feel worse now than a few minutes ago. Austin Reeder was a class *A* jerk, just like she'd thought earlier when she'd asked him about his relationship with Kalama. Why her instincts had led her in the wrong direction, she'll never know.

Closing her eyes, her body shook. She wanted to cry over the mistake she'd made, but she couldn't. Soon she'd leave this elevator, and she didn't need anyone seeing her this distraught and asking questions.

She wiped the smudged mascara from underneath her eyes. As shame continued to grow inside her, she became more determined to find the evidence needed to put Austin Reeder in prison for murdering Kalama Kane. Men like Austin should be locked up forever.

The ding of the elevator announced the lobby of the Imperial Hawaiian Grand Hotel as it opened the doors for her. Taking a deep breath, she tried to rid herself of the proof she carried of her steamy kiss with Austin.

As her high heels clicked on the marbled floor, she focused on the front doors. She couldn't get out of this place fast enough. But when a man came rushing through, she paused. He saw her and stopped. His gaze swept over her from the top of her messy head clear down to her high-heeled shoes.

Kurt gasped, stroking his brown, well-groomed beard. "Talia Russell? Why do you look so... gorgeous?"

Growling, she slugged her partner in the arm. "Where have you been? I called you several times. Didn't you get my messages?"

He rubbed his shoulder and grimaced. "No, I haven't listened to your messages, yet. I figured you were calling me to tell me about the sergeant's instructions, which of course, I'd already heard. And I was in a hurry to change my clothes so I could meet you here."

"You changed?" She glanced over his attire, looking exactly the same as he did every day they had worked together in the past year. Today he wore navy blue slacks, and a beige, button-down shirt that had the sleeves rolled up to the elbow, and a blue, white, and black striped tie. Sometimes he wore a suit jacket that matched the slacks, sometimes he didn't. Today, he didn't.

"Of course. You didn't expect me to come here wearing my sweats, did you?" He shrugged. "I was jogging when the sergeant called."

She groaned. "I can't believe you went home and changed your clothes. The sergeant wouldn't let me do that. I was at my father's engagement party."

Kurt chuckled as he eyed her dress, once again. "You went and talked to Reeder looking this hot?"

She rolled her eyes and walked past him out of the hotel's automatic front doors. Several times throughout the year they'd been teamed up together, she had wanted to punch him in the nose. Now was one of those times. He enjoyed teasing her, which she could dish right back, but she wasn't in the mood for it. Not after what had happened with Austin.

"Did you find out anything when you talked to Reeder?" he asked, keeping up with her long strides.

"A little."

"Tell me."

"Reeder is definitely a suspect. He was carrying on with Kalama before she was murdered."

"Carrying on? Do you mean they were lovers?"

She rolled her eyes again, and this time she glanced at him. "Reeder didn't consider them lovers because there was no love between them."

Kurt shook his head. "What does that mean?"

Once she reached her silver Volkswagen Jetta, she stopped and leaned against it. "I'll tell you about it later. Right now, I want to go home and change. My feet are killing me. I'll meet you back at the station in an hour, and I'll explain more at that time."

She didn't wait for his answer before climbing in and shutting the door. Kurt waited a few moments before he turned and walked to his dark blue Honda Accord. She started her car and drove out of the parking lot, feeling lower than dirt.

She'd treated Kurt badly. Of course, they all had their bad days, and she was always there to help lift Kurt's spirits, just as he'd been there to lift hers. But not today. Nothing could cheer her up. Maybe if she could go back in time to right after getting the call from Sergeant Feakes, she'd certainly do things differently. First off, she'd go home to change instead of being afraid that the sergeant might reprimand her for wasting her time as he'd told her before. Then, she wouldn't have acted unprofessionally.

This wasn't the first time she'd pretended to be someone else in order to obtain the answers she sought, and it wouldn't be the last time, but it was the only time she'd forgotten that she was a police detective. She'd somehow forgotten that Austin Reeder was a suspect.

For some reason, she saw him as a handsome, charming man who was actually interested in dating her. That, of course, led her into massaging his neck, and having him kiss her hand. The sultry way he'd looked at her when she fell on his lap also melted her completely, and heaven help her, but she'd wanted to know what it felt like to be kissed by someone so handsome.

Tears streamed from her eyes as she drove toward home. How could she hold her head up now? And how was she supposed to tell Kurt what she'd done?

She was such an idiot... an idiot who'd pretended to be a girl for hire, which was what he'd thought she was. Could she sink any lower than that?

FIVE

Austin wiped the steamed mirror in the bathroom. He'd taken a nice hot and relaxing shower, but what he should have done was taken a very cold shower. Perhaps that would make him more alert this morning.

Once the mirror cleared and he could see his reflection, he frowned. As tired as he'd been, he slept restlessly, and it was all Talia's fault. Or perhaps, it was Ariki's fault. His friend had set Austin up when he had specifically asked Ariki not to. Because of that, and the way the date had ended, Austin hadn't been able to sleep.

Could Talia have been Ariki's birthday joke? Austin wouldn't have put it past his friend. But one way or another, he needed to know now. He also needed to find Talia and apologize.

As Austin dressed, his mind replayed everything that had happened yesterday with her, and one question stood out more than the others. If she hadn't been from Ariki, then why had she come to see him? And why was the door opened as she had mentioned? He'd locked the door before going in to take a shower, hadn't he? But he'd been so tired, it was likely he'd forgotten.

With a deep sigh, he groaned. He needed to talk to Ariki, today if possible. Lately, the women Ariki found for Austin had been all right, but there was nothing spectacular about them. He wasn't interested in a serious relationship. The type of women he dated were mainly one-night stands. But his friend had mentioned playing a joke on him...

Austin fisted his hands. Was Talia the joke? Was she sent here to get him interested enough to want to see her again, and again, and again? Curse Ariki if that was his plan.

Without wanting them to, old feelings resurfaced. Emotions he had buried years ago were peaking over the horizon, making him remember what it had felt like to have his heart trampled on. Gnashing his teeth, he thought back on his painful past.

Hadn't he learned not to become enthralled with a woman the way he was with wanting to find Talia so badly? Women were not worth getting emotional over. Not only did his fiancée teach him this painful lesson several years ago, but his very own mother had proven to him that women could never be trusted.

Austin's brain must have been running on empty yesterday due to exhaustion. That's the only reason he'd acted in such a way with Talia. But then she had made him feel things he'd never felt with the other women Ariki had set him up with. Talia had presented herself as someone who was shy and naive, and he'd suddenly wanted to be her protector.

He wrapped the tie around his neck and proceeded to loop it together as he stared in the full-length mirror in his room. Once again, images of Talia haunted him. She'd kissed him so passionately, how could he forget such an earth-shattering moment? Her long, black hair glided like silk against his fingers, and her amazing rusty brown eyes had darkened mere seconds before they'd kissed.

She'd certainly accomplished making him feel so much desire for her in such a short amount of time. He'd had his share of women over the past fifteen years, but none of them had stayed on his mind as Talia had. The question was, why?

He'd thought she was different, but he couldn't put his finger on what exactly made her that way. A smile tugged on his lips. Immediately after meeting her, he could tell she was more refined, mainly by her actions. He wanted another chance to be in her charming presence, and he definitely wanted to sample her sultry kisses again. No way could he let that beautiful woman hate him.

Pursuing Talia would be a challenge, but one he was willing to take on. He needed a little excitement in his life, and this would definitely be the key.

He grabbed his keys, his cell, and his wallet, and then headed downstairs. During the ride on the elevator, he realized he couldn't wait to talk to Ariki. He must call him now.

Austin dialed his friend's number and waited for him to answer.

The other line clicked on. "This is Ariki."

"Hey, it's Reeder. I want to thank you for your birthday gift."

There was a lengthy pause on the other end of the phone instead of the laughter Austin had expected.

"What birthday gift are you talking about?"

Austin chuckled. "You know what I'm talking about. I have to admit, though, she's one sensual woman. I'm surprised you didn't keep her for yourself."

"Reeder, I'm serious. I don't know what you're talking about."

Confusion filled his head. "I'm talking about Talia, the woman you sent me yesterday."

"I didn't send you a woman."

"Quit joking. I know she came from you. In fact, she told me you had sent her."

"Reeder, I don't have any women friends named Talia."

The elevator doors opened, and Austin walked into the underground parking. His nearly new, cherry red, Porsche was parked in his normal space. "She's about five foot, four inches tall. Her body is very slender, but toned. Her eyes are brown and she has long, black hair."

"Are you kidding me? You described most women I've met on the island," Ariki snipped. "Reeder, I promise, I didn't send anyone to you. You told me not to because of your business deal, so I didn't."

Finally, Austin realized his friend was telling the truth. His gut clenched and confusion filled his head. "How can that be?" he shouted as he clicked open his car and climbed in. "She was at my place yesterday. I asked her if you sent her and she said yes."

"She's lying! I didn't send her. I swear it."

Austin closed the door and started his car. "If you didn't send her, who did?"

"Did she say she was there as your birthday gift?"

As he backed out of the parking space, his mind tried to recall her specific words. "I think so."

"Man, I don't know what to say. She didn't come from me."

Austin gritted his teeth. This couldn't be right. Did he dream what had happened yesterday? No, he'd tasted her sweet lips all night long, and her lilac scent still clung to his robe.

"Well, I want to find her. I won't rest unless I know what she was doing in my penthouse apartment." He gripped the steering wheel tighter. "Ariki, I know you can find her. I don't know what it is about you, but you have a woman-radar."

Silence stretched on the other end of the phone. Austin waited for his friend to answer. During the wait, he tried to think of some bribes for his friend just in case he said no. Finally, a ragged sigh came from Ariki.

"Fine. I'll try and find her, but I need you to describe her the best you can. Tell me any of the outward flaws or interesting features she may have that will help me notice her."

A smile stretched across Austin's mouth. He couldn't help it. Thinking about her, made him this way. "She's very beautiful. Her wavy, jet black hair, tumbles over her shoulders to her lower back, and she has the most amazing brown eyes I've ever seen. Her hands are immaculately delicate with trimmed nails, but not the fake kind women like to wear nowadays. She's probably in her mid-twenties, and she's about five foot, four inches tall, with very shapely legs. Her chest is not too large, yet not too small. And her body is toned like she works out a lot."

Ariki chuckled. "But that could describe a thousand girls."

"No, Talia is one in a million. Her lips are slightly pouty, just the way a man likes just before he devours them, and she has a cute little button nose. Although her eyes are brown, they're really not quite that color, but almost rusty instead."

"Rusty?"

Austin's smile widened the longer he pictured her. "I know it sounds funny, but when you see her, you'll see what I'm talking about."

"Is there anything else?"

"No, I think I've covered every inch of her. When she came to see me, she wore a red and white floral dress. The short sleeves hung off her shoulders, and the dress was short, showing off her shapely legs. Her hair had been pulled back in a bun. She looked like she was going to some fancy party. I don't know if that will help you to find her, but that's about all of it in a nutshell."

"Thanks. Although I still expect it will be difficult to find her, I promise I'll try really hard. I suppose I owe you one since I didn't get you a birthday present."

Austin chuckled. "Thanks, Ariki."

After Austin hung up, he thought about what he'd just said. Had he really sounded like a love-struck boy just now? Of course, somehow he'd led the poor woman astray, and he wanted a second chance at passion.

Unbeknownst to him, the woman had gotten under his skin, and he actually liked the feeling. But he couldn't get soft at this crucial point in his life. Especially not now, since he'd be signing the papers to purchase a chain of resorts across the Pacific Islands tomorrow. He needed to stay focused and strong, and then after everything was over, he could let the eagerness fill him again.

Today was already starting out good, and hopefully he'd have some better news after work.

SIX

Talia took a fortifying breath as she smoothed out the tiny wrinkles from the fresh black slacks and lavender blouse she'd dressed in. This time she looked presentable to go to work. Although she'd told Kurt she'd meet him back at the station in one hour last night, her headache had grown worse, and she just couldn't attempt to talk to him – or anyone – about what had happened with Austin Reeder. The moments of pleasure she'd had with Austin were too embarrassing, and she couldn't face anyone.

However, today was a new day. She'd try to forgive herself for lapsing momentarily into stupidity with Austin, and start over. Now as she stood at the cement stairs leading into Honolulu's police station, she hoped her body didn't somehow magnify her transgression from the night before. Did she still look like a woman who'd just experienced the best kiss of her life? More importantly, did she look like someone who was very much ashamed of being attracted to a murder suspect?

As she walked into the building, her co-workers looked up at her, nodded a greeting, and then returned to their work. So far, so good. Meeting Kurt this morning would be different, she was sure.

He'd been on his computer when she walked into the room. His eyes were fixed on the monitor, and he absentmindedly twirled a lock of brown hair around a finger. She'd always liked to tease him about it doing this, but today she just wasn't in the teasing mood.

He didn't notice her until she was almost to her desk. When his gaze met hers, he pushed away from his desk and stood. His tall frame stood over her by a good five inches.

"How are you feeling?"

She gave him a one-shoulder shrug. "Better, I think."

"Are you ready to tell me what happened?"

She really wasn't, but… she had to tell him at some point. "Yes."

"Here?" He pointed to their desks. "Or somewhere in private?"

She took a quick glance around the room. There were too many people at their desks and could overhear. "Private."

He motioned her to step ahead of him, and then they walked into the nearest empty interrogation room. As she sat, he closed the door.

"Tell me what happened. I don't want you to leave anything out." Kurt paced in front of her. His tone of voice was the one he used when cross-examining the perps.

"Kurt," she said with a sigh. "I'm not a perp. I'm your partner, remember?"

He chuckled and sat across from her. "Fine. Is this better?"

"Much better." She forced a smile as she expelled a disheartened sigh. "I waited for you to meet me at the hotel, but as I waited outside of his penthouse suite, I heard a thump from inside. Because the front door was ajar, my gut told me to go in and check it out. I worried there was a robbery in progress, or worse… that someone was trying to kill him."

Kurt nodded. "I would have probably done the same thing."

"Good. Thankfully, it wasn't a robbery in progress, or someone trying to end his life. But he walked out of the bathroom wearing nothing but a bathrobe."

As she explained, she left out a few things, mainly because she didn't want Kurt to know all the nitty-gritty details like how incredibly handsome Austin was, and how sweet he seemed at first, and how her heart skipped a beat whenever he locked gazes with her. She especially didn't want Kurt to know how she'd lost control over her mind and actions when he had kissed her hand.

Kurt sucked in a fast breath. "What?" His voice lifted. "He thought you were a call girl?"

She shrugged. "What else was I to think? The questions he aimed at me led me to believe that I was being paid for by some guy named Ariki or Mr. Reeder, himself. Regardless, a *payment* was mentioned." She huffed. "And of course, you forget what I was wearing. It's no wonder he thought I was a hooker."

Kurt shook his head. "Hookers are different than call girls. I thought you knew that."

She scowled. "Well, yesterday when I was placed in that situation, I didn't see a difference."

Kurt's mouth quirked, but thankfully, he didn't laugh. She would have slugged him hard if he had.

"So, the only thing you found out about Kalama Kane was that she and Reeder were involved in a relationship?"

"Yes, I think. He mentioned knowing her, but they were just friends. He dropped the subject after that and wouldn't answer any more questions. When I tried to bring it back up, he… um, well, he tried to dissuade me from talking about it. I left there upset that he thought of me as a call girl, and of course, that I couldn't get him to talk."

"Perhaps if he thought you were a police detective, that wouldn't have happened."

She silently growled. "Hamill, you know as well as I do that suspects are more open with people who aren't connected with the police. Or have you forgotten that?"

"Now, now." He held up his hands in surrender. "There's no need to get irate with me."

She took a deep breath and slowly released it as she counted to ten. It was true, she was getting upset, but Kurt didn't have anything to do with it so she shouldn't take it out on him.

Her partner left his side of the table and walked around to her, sitting on the desk right beside her.

"I'm sure you know Mr. Reeder has a reputation with women, right?"

She folded her arms and lifted her chin. "I think he's an egotistical, male chauvinistic jerk, and if I ever see him again, it'll be too soon."

Kurt groaned and rubbed his forehead. "Really? Most women I know fall madly in love with him, or his money, at first sight."

"Well, I'm not like most women." She really hated lying, but she detested looking like a fool, even more.

He frowned. "I'm sorry to hear that."

"Why?" she hesitantly asked.

"Because yesterday while Gibbs and Tyrone were investigating the victim's apartment again, you'll never guess what they found."

"What?"

Kurt pushed his fingers through his thick wavy hair that almost brushed his shoulders. It was getting long, and he needed it cut.

"They found several receipts from a drugstore, where she'd purchased contraceptives and hygiene items. Not only that, she had a monthly prescription of birth control pills."

Talia shrugged. "Kalama was a woman who likes to be extra careful. After all, she was seeing Romeo Reeder."

Kurt chuckled. "There's more. They asked the neighbors if she had any boyfriends, and nobody saw her with anyone. Gibbs and Tyrone discovered that she had made large deposits in her bank account in the last two years." He arched an eyebrow. "They showed Kalama's picture to the store manager, and he said she'd been a regular customer for about two years." He licked his lips. "And didn't you just tell me Reeder said he'd known Kalama from his past?"

"Yes, he said that."

"Don't you see, Talia?" Kurt stood and placed his hand on her shoulder. "Kalama had been a girl for hire these last two years. That explains the expensive jewelry and the contraceptives."

Talia gasped. "No wonder Romeo had mentioned paying me last night. And Ariki must be involved, too. Reeder talked about his friend getting him women all the time."

Disgrace swept through her, churning her stomach, just as it had done yesterday. For years, she'd tried not to look like a floozy in front of men. She'd wanted them to see her for her mind, not her other attributes. Now she felt almost as low as women like Kalama.

Talia didn't know how she could remove this feeling, but she needed to do it, soon. She couldn't work this way.

"All right, so Kalama was a girl for hire." Talia cocked her head. "What does this have to do with me seeing Romeo again?"

He laughed and sat on the edge of the table again. This time, he took her hand loosely in his and gently stroked her fingers. The only time Kurt got mushy like this was when he desperately wanted something. He'd even gone as far as to bat his big hazel eyes and pout. How pathetic. She definitely didn't want to hear what he had to say, only because she knew she'd lose her breakfast all over him.

"Well, I got to thinking, since Reeder thinks you were hired by Ariki, you could play along until you get him to confess."

She narrowed her gaze on her partner, who she was seriously thinking of making him her *ex-partner* now. Her heartbeat hammered wildly. "Do you honestly believe Reeder is guilty?"

Kurt's hesitation made her nervous, but finally he gave her a slow nod. "Actually, I do. Reeder is a rich guy, and I'm sure a lot of people try to blackmail him in attempts to get some of his money. The other men on the list that was in Kalama's robe pocket were also wealthy, but not even close to making what Reeder does. Reeder moves from woman to woman quickly, and that tells me that he doesn't care about what happens to his victims. Women like Kalama are expendable to men like him."

"But what's his MO?"

Once again, Talia could see the wheels turning inside her partner's head as he paused in deep thought. He kept his gaze on her. This man was easy to read. Of course, working closely with him, she learned how to understand his expressions.

Finally, his eyes widened and he grinned. "I'm willing to bet money Kalama was going to blackmail him. Powerful men in the community like the men on her list would be an easy target to blackmail."

Talia nodded. "Yes, I believe you're correct."

"So? Does that mean you'll go undercover and play the woman he thinks you are?"

Frustration rose inside of her quickly, and she balled her hands. Her first instinct was to turn him down, but deep down, she knew he was correct. She'd have to find a way to be around that man without feeling any lower than she felt already.

"Fine, but I will not do what those women, um... do. There's no way I'll sink that low. Not for the job... not for anyone."

Kurt's expression relaxed. He winked and playfully punched her shoulder. "I don't expect you to. In fact, we'll figure out a way to make sure that doesn't happen."

She blew out a defeated breath of air. "Will Feakes go along with this?"

Kurt nodded. "I'll convince him that this is the best course of action."

"Good, because I don't think the sergeant likes me very much."

She stood and folded her arms across her chest, mainly to keep the dread from shivering inside her. "You got my back?"

"Don't I always?" He cupped her face with both hands. "You can count on me. I'll never let you down."

SEVEN

Talia leaned against the kitchen counter as she waited for her toast to pop out of the toaster. Yawning, she drummed her fingernails on the counter. She hadn't slept very well last night, and Austin had everything to do with it. She growled. That man disturbed her in her sleep just as much as when she was awake.

A hard knock rattled the door, making her jump. Who could be visiting in the morning? It must be someone who didn't know she worked for a living.

She moved to the door and looked through the peephole. The face on the other side surprised her. What was Kurt doing here? Curious, she hurried and opened the door. Her partner smiled at her.

"Hey," he said.

"Aloha," she replied hesitantly.

"I'm glad you're not still in bed." He walked into her apartment and she shut the door.

"You should know me by now. I'm an early bird."

He chuckled. "That's true, you are. It usually takes me two cups of coffee before I'm awake."

"Would you like me to make you some?" Kurt knew she didn't drink coffee, but her father did, as well as some of her friends, so she always had ground beans and a coffee maker on hand for when the occasion called for it.

"No, I'm good. I've already had some this morning. I needed to think on my way here."

"Kurt? Why are you here?"

He laughed loudly. "You act as if I don't ever come to your apartment."

"Kurt, you don't usually come in the morning."

He shrugged. "I thought we should discuss our plan for contacting Mr. Reeder today."

Inwardly, she groaned. Wasn't it enough that she hadn't been able to get that man off her mind since meeting him? Why did Kurt have to bring attention to the billionaire when what she really wanted was to forget him?

"Do we have to discuss it?" She rubbed the dull ache quickly forming in her forehead. She moved into the living room before plopping down on the loveseat.

Kurt joined her on the sofa and tapped his hand against her knee. "Yes. It's necessary to talk this out. We can't do anything to mess up our plans."

"I understand." She nodded, taking in a deep breath. "So how do you think I should meet him?"

"I was thinking," Kurt sat back against the sofa and draped his arm behind Talia, "that because you left so abruptly during your first meeting, you should return to his hotel, and—"

"Bad idea!" She shook her head as her heart pounded frantically. "I was quite insulted that he hinted about paying me for being his date, and I don't think—"

"But you need to earn his trust," Kurt cut in. "You won't be able to earn his trust if you happen to run into him on the street and strike up a conversation, you know."

Talia gnashed her teeth. She hated when he was right. His hazel gaze stayed on her for a few awkward silent moments. It was almost as if he waited for her to agree with him. She blew out a rushed breath. "Fine. I'll go to his hotel, but what kind of excuse should I give him?"

Kurt's energetic smile widened. "Oh, you're going to like this one." He winked. "You're going to tell him you think you left your purse there."

"Nope. It won't work. He knows I had it with me. I never even put it down since it had my Glock and badge in it."

Kurt muttered a cuss. "Are you sure?"

"Of course, I'm sure. He was trying to stop me, remember?"

"Hmm…" he rubbed his trimmed beard. "Maybe you could say you had come back to collect payment—"

Gasping, she slugged him in the arm. "You've got to be kidding. I'm not going to do that. Not after the way I ran out of there as if the devil was nipping at my heels."

He groaned and rested his head back against the couch. When he closed his eyes, silence stretched between them. She couldn't stop herself from gazing over him. From the first day she'd met him, she thought he was one good-looking man, but even back then, she knew not to judge a person by their appearance. However, the more she'd gotten to know him, the more she liked him. Kurt was easy to like. He entertained everyone in the precinct, especially her. For a few months, she thought she was developing a crush on him. She fought it as hard as she could. It wasn't a good idea to date a co-worker. Then, when they became partners, she definitely knew she needed to start thinking differently about him. So, he was like a brother to her. At least that's what she tried to believe.

"What other excuse could you use?" Kurt asked, lifting his head and looking at her. "I really don't see any other way to meet him again, unless we go as ourselves, and you know he's not going to be truthful with a cop."

Talia mentally shook away her thoughts of the past and focused once more on their conversation. "True. He wouldn't be truthful with me if that happened. He'd say I purposely tricked him because I was wearing that dress."

Chuckling, Kurt ruffled her hair. "You did look sexy."

"Knock it off," she slapped his hand away. Heat started climbing up her neck, making its way to her face, but she tried breathing normally and not getting too excited by his comment so that the blush wouldn't reach her cheeks.

His gaze locked with hers as his laughing subsided. She didn't want to read too much into this moment, but why were his hazel eyes softening? Even the lines in his face weren't as dominant.

A lump formed in her throat, and she swallowed hard. She prayed he didn't have *those* kinds of feelings for her. A relationship with her partner was not a good thing.

Suddenly, his eyes widened, and his smile grew. He straightened. "I think I have the answer."

What answer was he talking about? Her mind quickly replayed their conversation. Oh, yah, they were back on Austin Reeder. "It had better be good."

"You are going to return to his hotel to tell him that you were sorry for the way you acted."

She arched an eyebrow. "Excuse me? You want me to do what?"

"Just listen to me."

He took her hand in his and gently rubbed her fingers. Now she knew he was going to tell her something she wouldn't like.

"You're going to explain to Austin Reeder," Kurt continued, "how sorry you were for acting that way. Let him know you don't usually do… um, *that*, but you desperately needed the money."

Anger built inside of her again, and she tried to take her hand away, but he gripped onto it harder, making it impossible for her to release. "Kurt Hamill…" She usually only used his full name when she was upset.

"Listen to me before you interrupt." He smiled sweetly. "As I was saying, the reason you're doing this is to make him think you're new at this… um, kind of thing. That would explain why you acted the way you did the other day. He, of course, will have sympathy for you, and allow you to apologize."

When he paused, she quickly spoke before he could go on. "And why exactly would I be desperate for money?"

"I don't know." He shrugged. "Make up a story. Maybe you are looking for work and nobody will hire you. Maybe your father is sick and dying, and you need the money to pay for his medical expenses."

Thankfully, Talia's mind was working better now. "Okay, so tell me, oh master of all knowledge, how would I have known to go to Austin Reeder?"

Slowly, Kurt shook his head, but he still wore his cocky grin. "Because Kalama Kane recommended him as the man who could help you."

Talia gradually processed this information, and after a few awkward, silent seconds, she realized she couldn't think of anything to argue about. Perhaps Kurt's idea would work after all, and maybe she'd finally get some answers out of the good-looking womanizer.

* * * *

Kurt watched Talia carefully. He knew her well enough to know her moods, and at times, he even knew what she was thinking. Right now he saw a mixture of frustration and awe on her pretty, wide-eyed expression. He couldn't blame her for being upset. If roles were reversed, he'd be irate at her for suggesting such a thing. But Talia could definitely pull this off. She had the right body and looks. Not that he'd ever paid for one, but he'd seen movies. And being a police detective, he'd seen his share, as well.

If anyone could play this part, Talia could. She wouldn't take crap from Austin Reeder, either. Of course, Kurt wouldn't let the perp lay a hand on his partner. He'd told her once that he'd protect her, and he'd move Heaven and Hell to make sure she was taken care of.

She released a heavy breath and her body relaxed. He still held her hand, and even her tight grip had diminished.

"So," she said softly, "how are we going to do this? How are we going to keep me from really playing the part of a call girl?"

He smiled and squeezed her hand gently. "I've already figured this out. I'll get us the ear pieces, and we'll both wear them. That way, if I can hear the perp is getting out of control, I'll come rescue you."

A small grin touched her mouth. "Rescue me? Kurt, really, when do I need rescuing?"

"You know what I mean. I know you'll be able to take the perp down, because I've seen you do it many times. But I just want you to know I'll be there as your backup."

"That's just fine, but you really didn't answer my question. What is going to keep me from performing? If Reeder thinks I'm a call girl, and tries to... do things, what excuse can I give him that will make him stop?"

Kurt scratched his chin, trying to think up some kind of excuse. Nothing came to mind. "I don't know. I'm not a woman. What excuses do you usually give men?"

"Augh!" Talia rolled her eyes and pushed him aside as she stood. "Sometimes, Kurt, you make me want to punch you in the face."

He laughed and rose to his feet. "But you still love me, right?" He winked.

She shook her head and walked toward the back room.

"Hey? Where are you going?" he asked.

"I have to find clothes so I can look the part, don't I?"

"Come on. We don't want to be late for work."

As he walked behind her, he grinned. She was definitely a looker. Any man would be blind not to notice how sexy Talia was even when she tried not to be. When he'd first been paired with her, he went to the sergeant to persuade him to change his mind because he didn't want to be attracted to his partner. That didn't make a good working environment. But the sergeant turned down Kurt's request. Over the months, he fought the attraction, and finally became comfortable with her. It was still hard not to think how gorgeous she was, but his job was important, and having a trusted partner was even more important. He didn't want to ruin that between them.

But now with her undercover assignment, he wasn't sure he liked it even if he had suggested it. Although he knew she could pull it off, he still worried that the perp might get out of hand being around an attractive woman like Talia. Kurt wouldn't hesitate in shooting the perp if that ever happened.

EIGHT

Talia adjusted the tight, black skirt around her thighs, and smoothed a hand down the snug fitting, stretchy blue shirt with elbow-length sleeves. She kept a few buttons of the shirt open at her throat, knowing it didn't show much of what a man wanted to see. She left her hair long, and she placed a Frangipani flower behind her right ear. The other ear was covered with her hair, and hid the earpiece she wore.

As she watched the numbers of the floors click higher on the elevator's wall panel as it counted toward the penthouse suite, she touched her finger to the earpiece. "I hope you can hear me," she said softly.

"I can." Kurt's voice came across loud and clear. "And just relax. You look gorgeous."

Inwardly, she groaned. She didn't need to hear that. "Thanks, Hamill. I'm happy you approve of my Halloween costume."

His laughter from the other end made her smile, but it didn't relax her at all. What worried her more than coming face to face with Austin again was knowing that Kurt could now hear their conversation. Her gut twisted. She hadn't told Kurt about the kiss she shared with the perp, and if she had it her way, Kurt would never find out. It was degrading enough that she'd lowered herself and allowed Austin to seduce her into a passionate kiss. She couldn't allow it to happen again.

The elevator doors opened and she stepped into the hallway, wearing her black, high-heeled stilettos. Shoulders back, chin lifted, she walked toward the familiar door as her heart frantically beat against her ribs. Good grief, if the noise from her heartbeat was any louder, the first floor would be able to hear.

Her stomach twisted in knots, making its own pretzels. She tried to breathe slower in hopes that it would calm her down, but her fast pulse let her know nothing would be coming to a stop anytime soon. She may as well be running a 4k race. If her heart was going to get exercise, her legs should, as well.

Taking a deep breath for courage, she raised her hand and knocked. Then waited. There was nothing but silence from the other side of the door. She hesitated a couple more seconds before knocking again. Still nothing. Was he taking another shower? Well, she wasn't about to go inside this time just to find out. Not even if he slipped and fell on the wet floor.

"I don't think he's home," she said so Kurt could hear her.

"The hotel clerk told me Mr. Reeder would be in his suite this afternoon."

She shrugged. "Maybe he's resting, then."

"Knock harder."

Irritated, she did as Kurt requested and knocked harder. Still, there was no sound on the other side.

"I think the hotel clerk was wrong," she said.

"Yeah, it looks that way to me, too."

She moved back to the elevator and walked inside. She pressed the button of the floor she wanted. There was no use waiting around here. When the doors closed, she released a sigh of relief. And yet, inevitably, she would have to meet up with the perp sometime, and then she'd have to talk to him.

"He's not here, so I'm coming down."

Kurt grumbled. "We'll try again later."

"Yes, we will."

"I'm shutting down my earpiece now."

"Me, too." She reached to her ear just as the elevator doors opened on the seventh floor. She scooted to the corner, readying for others to join her on her ride down. But only a single man walked in. A very familiar, single man.

When Austin Reeder's gaze met hers, he gasped and froze in his step. She groaned in silence, leaving the earpiece where it was, just in case. What was he doing on the seventh floor instead of up in his own suite?

His eyes widened. "It's you!"

Apparently, her acting must begin now, not later. She licked her lips and moistened her suddenly dry throat with a hard swallow. "Aloha. Yes, it's me."

"What are you doing here?" he asked as he came inside and pressed the key to the second floor.

"I, um…" *Are you kidding me? Tongue-tied again? This is definitely not like you, Russell! Get a grip!* She cleared her throat. "I'm actually here to see you."

"Me?"

She couldn't tell for sure, but it appeared as though he held his breath. "Yes. I came to… apologize." She almost couldn't get that last word out. She really hated begging for forgiveness when none of this was her fault.

"You did? Why?"

"Well, you see—" The elevator dinged and the doors opened to the second floor.

Austin held the door open and motioned with his other hand. "Would you like to join me for a drink? There is a concierge lounge on this floor."

"Oh, yes. That would be nice." With any luck, other people would be there, too.

Austin waited until she walked beside him, and then he led them down the hall. When they entered the room, she quickly scoped it out… and groaned. They were the only ones here so far.

He moved behind the counter to pour them drinks. This time he didn't ask what she wanted, but she wouldn't drink alcohol, anyway. She'd just have to act like she was drinking, just as she'd done when they'd been in his room.

Within moments, he brought the drinks to the nearest table. She lowered herself to the chair, and he sat across from her. When his gaze met hers again, his green eyes twinkled. Why did they have to do that? Now the fluttering in her bosom had returned. Even her knees became weak.

"I must admit," he began, "I'm happy to see you. I haven't stopped thinking about you since you ran out of my suite."

Interesting. Why would he think about her? Maybe he felt guilty for frightening her and making her run. "Well, I'll admit that you have been on my mind quite a bit, too."

"Why?" He reached over and touched her hand resting on the table.

"Well, you see..." Stubbornness blocked the words from leaving her mouth. *Just say it!* "I wanted to apologize for what happened."

His eyes widened again. "Apologize? Why? I'm the one who should be apologizing."

Yes! But she had to appear as the martyr in this situation. "Because of the way I acted."

He took both of her hands in his. "Talia, you were frightened of me, I could tell. I should have tried harder to set your mind at ease. I'm not the monster you probably think I am." He chuckled. "Ask anyone. I could never harm a woman."

Talia's mind stalled. Why had he said that? Did he know she was really here to ask about Kalama's murder? What man goes around saying they don't hurt women?

She tried to smile. "I'm relieved to know that, but..." She took a deep breath. "I'm rather new at this, and well, I was being awkward for a reason."

He arched an eyebrow, but then his gaze narrowed on her. "You are new at what, exactly?"

Silently, she groaned. He was really going to make her spell it out? How humiliating! "You know... *it.*"

His expression changed to one of confusion. "It?" He shook his head. "Do you mean dating?"

She desperately wanted to roll her eyes and make some kind of sarcastic remark, but she refrained, though it was hard. So apparently, they call it dating now. "Well, I guess it's called dating."

"Talia, I'm not sure what you're saying." He took a drink of his brandy.

She glanced down at her glass. Too bad she wasn't a drinker, because now would be the perfect time to start. She expelled a frustrated breath. "You know, paying me for my services."

He choked and spit some of the liquor out of his mouth. Quickly, he snatched a napkin and dabbed the table where the liquid had landed before bringing the napkin to his face and wiping. Shaking his head, he cleared his throat. "You wanted me to pay you for that?"

Okay, so now she was confused. If he didn't think she was a girl for hire, then why did he say the things he did? "Well, isn't that what you'd said to me? Something about earning my pay?"

He groaned and closed his eyes as he rubbed his forehead. She didn't dare say anything more, not until he explained himself first. Wasn't it bad enough she was in this predicament?

Sighing, he looked at her as a frown claimed his face. "Talia, I'm very sorry for everything. I can't believe you actually thought that I wanted to pay you for your services."

"Then why did you say it?" she asked.

"Because I thought my friend Ariki was up to his old tricks again, and teasing me with one of his friends. I said that as a joke, meaning that Ariki was paying you to play this prank on me for my birthday."

"It was your birthday?" Surprise washed through her.

"Yes, but I was too exhausted to celebrate, and Ariki knew it. That's why I thought he'd sent you. And that's why I begged you to kiss me."

Mortification ran through her, and she wanted to dig a big hole and stick her head into it. She hadn't heard Kurt in her ear, so obviously, he'd really shut down. Perhaps that was a good thing, especially now. "Oh, wow. Now I'm the one who is embarrassed."

He scooted his chair closer to hers and took hold of her hand. "This was just all a mix-up, that's all. There's nothing to be embarrassed about." He paused, and during those seconds, his expression changed again. Lines appeared on his forehead and around his eyes. Even his lips thinned. "Talia? If Ariki didn't send you, then why did you come to see me?"

She tried to remain calm. After all, she and Kurt had discussed this part. She knew what to say, but now she was going to sound extremely foolish. But there was no other way, especially, if she needed to ask him about Kalama.

She cleared her throat. "I'd led you to believe that Ariki sent me, but the truth is, Kalama Kane recommended you."

Gasping, he released her and pulled back. "She recommended me? For what?"

"That you would be the one to help me."

Slowly, his head shook back and forth. "I still don't quite understand. Why would she send you to me?"

Here it comes… the shame of telling him such an unbelievable tale. "I'm desperate for money. I'd just lost my job, and I needed something to pay rent until something else came along. I'm about to be evicted. What am I going to do if that happens?" She raised her voice, laying it on thick. "I've never done this – this thing before, but Kalama mentioned that she had, and it helped her get the money she needed."

He nodded. "Go on."

"Anyway, Kalama said you could help me. That's why I came to see you the other day. I was very nervous. I didn't know what was going to happen. And then, after the kiss… well, I just couldn't do it. That's why I ran out the way I had."

Empathy glowed in his hypnotic green eyes. He stroked his thumbs over her knuckles so very tenderly, she could have melted right off the chair and to the floor.

"I'm sorry you had to go through that. Kalama shouldn't have sent you to me. She knew better." He shook his head. "You see, a few years ago, I had helped her when she was down on her luck. She was working for a place called Belle's Escort Service, and Kalama was in over her head. A few months ago, she came back and needed money to start her own business. It had something to do with creating a clothing line. I can't remember. Anyway, I gave her a little money, and she was upset that I hadn't given her more, so she stormed out, muttering threats under her breath, and I've not seen her since."

Although this whole conversation was humiliating, at least she was getting him to talk. But then… why wasn't Kurt hearing any of this?

"Oh, Austin. I feel so foolish now." She lowered her head, laying on the drama. "Kalama took advantage of my stressful situation, and I'm ashamed I fell for her lies. She made me think that you would... well, you know." To add to her Academy Award acting, she lifted a hand to her mouth as if she was holding back a sob.

"Don't blame yourself, Talia."

He scooted his chair closer and wrapped his arms around her. She rested her head on his chest. Inhaling deeply had been a huge mistake. Oh, why did he have to smell so good?

"Talia? Are you there? What's going on?"

Kurt's voice in her ear startled her, and she snapped upright. Another big mistake, because now she was looking at the very irresistible, Austin Reeder, right in the face. If there were two inches between them, she'd be lucky. She prayed he hadn't heard Kurt's voice since she was still in his arms.

"What's wrong?" Austin asked.

"I, um... Well, I just don't want you to think this is your fault at all." Her mind scrambled for words. "This was Kalama's sick joke, and that's all."

"Sick joke?" Kurt asked in a lower voice this time. "What did I miss?" He swore. "I knew I should have kept my earpiece in."

"Yes, it was." Austin stroked her cheek. "And so, I don't want you to feel guilty, either. She knew what kind of man I was, and she took advantage of me, too. Apparently, Kalama enjoyed playing with people's lives."

Talia nodded. "Can you forgive me? I was just so... desperate. Now I realize how wrong I was."

A slow smile stretched across his face. "There is nothing to forgive. But, how is your housing situation now? Are you going to get evicted? Because I don't want you thinking you have to find other men who will pay. I can give you a small loan until you find a new job."

Her heart wrenched with an unknown feeling. He would really do that to someone he'd only met once and who he'd shared an electrifying kiss with? Perhaps she'd judged him too harshly at first. Of course, knowing he didn't pay for women was a great relief, too.

"I – I – I don't know what to say, Austin. Why are you being so kind to me? I don't know when I'll be able to pay you back."

"Don't worry about that now. I just want you to rest assured that I'll help you in any way I can." His fingers moved to her bottom lip and traced underneath. "As long as you promise you'll not go into *that* type of career just to get quick money."

Her heartbeat quickened. The tone in his voice had changed, deepened, reminding her of how he'd sounded right before they had kissed. And the way he stared at her mouth let her know he was thinking about that, too. She couldn't let that happen. Especially, not with Kurt in her ear. "I promise."

Just when she thought Austin was going to place his lips on hers, he pulled away. Instead, he picked up his brandy and nearly gulped it down. She took this moment to breathe slower, hoping to regulate her heartbeat. She was glad he decided to withdraw first, because she seriously doubted she had the strength, even knowing Kurt would hear.

"I suppose I should go." She stood.

He quickly rose to his feet and grasped her hand. "Forgive me for being busy today. I just don't have much time to spend with you. However, I hope you are free for dinner later tonight. I'd really like to get to know you better."

Tell him no! "Uh, all right." *Way to go, Russell. You're such a coward sometimes.* But she tried to convince herself she needed more time to ask him about Kalama. It didn't matter what he'd told her earlier, he was still a suspect. However, his innocence was becoming clearer the more she got to know him. "Do you want to pick me up?" Her mind screeched to a halt. No! She couldn't have him knowing where she lived. "Or," she quickly added, "should I come here? I'm sure this hotel has a restaurant."

"Yes, it does." He winked. "Why don't you come here around seven o'clock."

She nodded and smiled. "Okay. It's a date."

Just thinking about it being a real date sent her mind into a frenzy, and her heart into overdrive.

NINE

Low burning candles and soft music from the Bluetooth speakers would set the mood for tonight's romance. Austin hadn't stopped thinking about his date with Talia, and he realized that he didn't want to take her to the restaurant. He'd rather take her on his private jet and fly her to Venice, Italy. But then he quickly squashed that idea since he wanted her to get to know him, not his money. Privacy was what they needed. If it was just the two of them, she'd open up to him a little easier. And maybe, just maybe, she'd let him kiss her again.

He adjusted the wine bottle in the bucket of ice sitting on the dinette table. He picked out the overlooked green leaf in the bowl of fresh strawberries before walking over and dimming the lights.

Before his anxiously-awaited guest arrived, he hurried into the bathroom to check his appearance one last time. As he slapped on his favorite cologne, he caught his reflection smiling like a little boy on Christmas day, but surprisingly enough, he couldn't control his eagerness.

He ran his hand over his wavy brown hair, knowing women liked this particular trait about him – hair just long enough to run their fingers through, yet not too long to get in the way. He glanced down at his gray, short sleeved polo shirt and debated whether to tuck it into the waist of his Levis or just wear it out. Then again, if he tucked it inside, she'd be able to see his muscular frame better. Grinning, he shoved the ends of the shirt into his Levis.

Showing off his pearly whites, he stepped closer to the mirror to inspect his teeth, making sure he'd brushed and flossed his teeth clean. Satisfied, he straightened. Everything had to be perfect tonight. This was his only chance to show Talia what a charming and gentle man he really was. If he failed again, she'd never come back.

His lucky stars were aligned perfectly tonight. He had a good feeling that things would turn out as planned. Talia had come back to him when he thought he'd never see her again, and he was determined not to let her go this time. He was relieved he'd stopped her from making a big mistake in following Kalama's advice. But it was strange to think that as many situations that he'd helped Kalama get out of, she was actually helping him this time.

The doorbell rang, and his heart sprang with excitement. Taking a deep breath to calm himself, he walked out of the bathroom and to the front door. He wiped his sweaty palms on his pants, chuckling to think he was so anxious. Austin Reeder? Nervous? Ridiculous. Wouldn't the press have a field day with this story?

When he received his first look at Talia, his heart melted. Instead of the sexy dresses she'd worn before, her attire was much different tonight. Instead, she wore a short sleeve, dark blue shirt that was buttoned down the front. She had on tan slacks that fit her figure perfectly. Nothing about her clothes could be considered sexy, and yet, he liked this casual look on her.

Her jet-black hair was left long, flowing like silk over her shoulders and down her back. His fingers itched to stroke her locks; to feel it brush across his face as he kissed her neck. A Hawaiian Hibiscus flower was stuck behind her ear, and the urge to lean in and smell the fragrance became overwhelming. He quickly stopped his thoughts before they got out of hand. This wasn't the way to start out the evening. But how could he not think that way?

Another thing different about her was that she didn't cake on her makeup as she'd done before. But whatever she'd done, it was perfect. It made Talia appear more natural. He liked that a lot, because now he knew she had natural beauty.

A black purse hung over her arm, and one hand clutched onto it so tight her fingers were white. The poor woman looked so nervous that she might empty her stomach at any moment. He'd change that. He'd have her relaxed in no time.

Giving her a tender smile, he stepped away from the door. "Good evening, Talia. Won't you come in?"

She nodded then walked past him into the suite. Her heavenly scent of lilacs wafted around him just like it had done the other night.

"How are you this evening?" He shut the door.

"I guess I'm a little nervous," she answered as her gaze swept through the room. "Uh, Austin? I thought we were going to the restaurant for dinner."

"We were, until I realized I like room service much better. It's not as crowded here, either." He smiled.

"Well, whatever we are having for dinner, smells Heavenly."

"I hope you like this." He glanced at the dinette table where the food was laid out. "I've ordered my favorite dish from the restaurant. We'll be having smoked duck breast, peach risotto, charred broccoli, heirloom carrots, and red wine shallots. For dessert, we'll have dark chocolate pudding."

Her expression relaxed as a small smile touched her face. "That sounds wonderful."

He motioned toward the table. "Shall we eat?"

She nodded, so he took her hand and brought her to the table, and like a true gentleman, pulled out the chair for her to sit.

Her eyes widened. "My, my... don't we have impeccable manners."

He laughed and sat beside her. "I'd like to believe so, since I was taught as a young boy how to treat a woman." Surprisingly enough, he wasn't taught that by his mother. He quickly quenched the horrible memories and focused back on his beautiful date.

"Not many men do that. My father drilled into my brothers that if they couldn't treat a woman kindly, they would not have satisfied marriages."

"Your father is very wise." He slipped his hand over hers and softly caressed her skin. "I hope your brothers took his advice."

She shrugged. "Only my oldest brother is married, and so far, he and his wife seem to be very happy. My other two brothers are in college. One wants to be a doctor, the other one, a lawyer."

"How impressive. I'm happy that they want to make something out of their lives."

"We all do. Even me." She sighed and frowned.

"What do you want to become? Or have you already reached that goal?"

He waited for her answer, but she seemed to squirm in her chair and play with her utensils. Hopefully, he hadn't asked the wrong question. Suddenly, he realized he had because she'd wanted to earn extra money being a call girl, and that right there hinted to him she didn't have a good profession.

Silently, he groaned. Now he needed to say something to make up for his blunder.

* * * *

Talia couldn't think. Why did this always happen to her when she was around this man? Had he some kind of hypnotic power to make all of the thoughts in her head disappear? So far, that's the only excuse she could come up with.

She couldn't necessarily tell him that she'd always wanted to be a cop or detective, because what kind of woman would do that and then try to be a call girl? Perhaps she'd tell him about the profession she'd almost gone into.

She raised her gaze and met his worried one. "I was actually in college to get a degree in interior design, but I had to drop out to care for my father when he became sick. Once he was feeling better, I found a job, but I wasn't making a lot of money. One thing led to another, and suddenly bills started piling up. Then my job laid me off, and well… now I'm here, looking really pathetic about now, I suppose."

Sadness encased his expression. He took her hands in his, once more. It was hard to admit, but when he did this, it calmed her.

"My sweet, Talia. You have such a caring heart to drop out of school to watch over your father. I think interior design would be a great career for you. I hope you return once you can get back on your feet."

She nodded. "That is my plan."

He released her and turned to grab one of the dishes of food. "We'd better eat before our food gets cold."

"Oh, yes. I'm starving."

It melted her heart to think he'd serve her. Most wealthy businessmen sat back and allowed others to serve them. Every minute with him, he amazed her more and more. Now she wondered how he could even be considered a suspect at all. He was so kind and attentive, and that definitely wasn't how murderers acted. There were people who had split personalities, but because he'd made it so far in life and was still going strong, that told her he didn't have that particular disorder.

As they ate their dinner, she relaxed and enjoyed listening to him. He talked about his hotels, and more importantly, how he'd obtained them. The idea of him being a murderer floated further from her mind. This man was extremely intelligent.

Off and on throughout the conversation, she could hear Kurt in her ear, making snide remarks. Obviously, her partner thought Austin was lying about everything. She was tempted to take Kurt out of her ear and enjoy her date for the rest of the night. But she knew she had to somehow get around to that important question… *what were you doing on the night of Kalama's murder?*

When there was a break in the conversation, she asked, "Austin, you really are a busy man, aren't you?"

"Yes." He took a sip of his wine. "That's one of the reasons I cherish times when I can relax, like right now."

"I wonder if that's the reason you weren't here when I first came by to talk to you." Talia tried not to pat herself on the back for coming up with this idea so quickly.

His drink stalled at his mouth. "You came to see me another time?"

"Yes. Let's see," she tapped her finger on her cheek, "today is Friday, so I came to see you last Sunday. It was around ten o'clock in the morning."

"Good girl, Russell," Kurt said in her ear. "That's the way to get Romeo to talk."

"Wow." Austin shook his head. "You were a determined woman, weren't you?"

"Like I said before. I was desperate." She paused, hoping he'd tell her where he was, but when he laid his hand over hers and gently squeezed, she wondered if he was going to thwart her question.

"Let's take our drinks over to the sofa." He stood and held her hand until she rose to her feet. With drinks in their hands, he led her to the furniture. "It's more comfortable over here."

She hardly tasted her wine, but only because she wanted a clear head tonight. He sat very close to her and placed their wine glasses on the wooden coffee table in front of them.

"Talia, I'm really worried about you. I know we only just met, but I care about you a great deal. Please don't lower yourself to become one of those girls like Kalama had been." He stroked her cheek. "You're much too intelligent for that."

He thinks I'm intelligent? Her heartbeat picked up in rhythm. "Austin, when I came to see you on Sunday," she tried to bring back that subject, "I was in a different frame of mind. Maybe it was a good thing you weren't here that morning."

He turned his body closer to hers and slid his arm across the back of the sofa. A grin tugged on his mouth. "Why? What would you have done if I was here?"

Well, at least he said something that let her know he wasn't home around that time of day when Kalama was murdered. However, she still didn't think that made him a suspect.

She chuckled and shook her head. "Oh, no. I don't dare say too much. Besides, I'm sure you can guess what would have happened. I'm assuming you wouldn't have been exhausted like you were the other night."

"No, I wouldn't have been exhausted." He leaned closer and took a lock of her hair, caressing its length. "But I would have wanted to get to know you anyway."

Kurt swore in her ear. "Are you kidding me? He's really going to revert back to that topic?"

"Why, Austin?" she asked, trying to ignore Kurt's voice. At this moment, she wished she wasn't wearing the earpiece. "Why would you have wanted to get to know me?"

"You're different." He shrugged. "I can't put my finger on it, but you're a mystery to me. At times I think you're just like those other women Ariki set me up with, but then you do or say something that throws me off. That makes me believe you are more special than the others."

She forced a small laugh, still trying not to allow him to completely melt her. "Austin, you still don't know me. Why do you say these things?" When he opened his mouth to reply, she placed her fingers on his lips, quieting him. "Because from life's experience, men who over-flatter me only want one thing. And well, I can't respect a man who is like that."

His gaze narrowed as he held her hand to his mouth. Slowly, he placed soft kisses on her fingertips. As she stared into his green eyes, they darkened with desire. Her heart hammered in a different rhythm, but it was not panic. She couldn't understand why she wasn't worried right now.

Gradually, he smiled. "And you are very smart to have figured that out so soon in life. But," he shook his head, "if I had felt that way about you when we first met, I wouldn't have acted on my urges. You see, I, too, have experienced love's hard lessons, and I guard my heart very carefully."

Was he just saying the words she wanted to hear, or was he being serious? Where were her gut feelings now when she needed them? "I see we have one thing in common."

"I'm sure we have more," his hand moved from her hair to her face, close to her mouth, "but we just need to discover what they are."

"And how you do you suggest we do that?" After she'd said it, she couldn't believe she was talking this way. Was she trying to seduce him? Nah, that couldn't be right.

"I have an idea." His voice softened as he leaned closer. His gaze stayed on her mouth.

She held her breath, waiting for the moment she'd feel the electricity buzzing through her from his passionate kiss. It could only be better this time, since she didn't think he was the murderer now.

As his lips touched hers, she closed her eyes. Warmth immediately spread through her, and she held back the sigh that was ready to release from her throat. But no, she couldn't let him know how severely her body reacted to his kiss.

"Talia," Kurt whispered. "What's going on? Why do I hear heavy breathing?"

She sighed, but it wasn't because of how pleasurable it was to kiss Austin. How could she have forgotten about Kurt?

She quickly pulled back and stared into Austin's surprised eyes. "I, um, I have a better idea." She licked her lips. "Let's, um… Do you arm wrestle?"

Austin's eyes widened even more. "Arm wrestle?"

Chuckling, she moved off the couch and back toward the table. "Yes. Arm wrestle. You'd be shocked how well one can get to know another person just by arm wrestling."

"Heehee," Kurt's voice rumbled from her ear. "Talia, you haven't changed a bit. I remember our first arm wrestle."

Inwardly, Talia growled. She didn't want Kurt in her ear. Not now. She wanted to get to know Austin so that she could make the final decision of whether he was a killer or not. With Kurt's words influencing her, she doubted she'd be able to think clearly.

Austin smiled and moved from the couch, coming toward her. "It's been a while since I've arm wrestled, but now seems like a good time."

She smiled, genuinely smiled, and her heart lifted. She finally felt she could handle any situation now. That's what she needed in order to crack this case. Although she was undercover, she wanted to be herself. And starting now, she'd do that.

TEN

Kurt boiled with anger as he sat downstairs in the bar, waiting for Talia to finish her date with Reeder and come join him. He didn't want to imagine what she and Romeo were doing upstairs in his penthouse suite. Kurt was able to listen to their conversation until about the time they started arm wrestling. Something must have happened to have the earpiece fall out of her ear, because after that, all he heard was muffling sounds. At first, he thought about going upstairs and making up some kind of story of why he needed to interrupt them, but when he heard them laughing at different times throughout the evening, he realized she was not in any harm.

Grumbling under his breath, he grasped the beer bottle and lifted it to his lips. He knew his partner well, and by now she was having doubts about Reeder being the perp. Men like Reeder knew how to sweet talk women. Men like Reeder were perfect liars. Their good looks, their charm, but mostly, their money would turn any woman's head.

Not for one second did Kurt believe Reeder was innocent. Unfortunately, he needed to find proof, because Talia would demand it. Talia would be hard to sway, especially if she allowed Reeder to kiss her.

Kurt tightened his fingers on the neck of the bottle, wishing it was someone's throat instead. If it was the last thing he did, he'd show Talia that Reeder was the murderer. Of course, sitting here, wallowing in his pity wasn't helping matters. But he couldn't do anything until he knew she was all right. He had to make sure she didn't spend the night in the penthouse of love...

There had been nothing but silence on the other end of his earpiece, and that worried Kurt. That could only mean one thing. She and Reeder were kissing.

He swore and took another gulp of beer. He raked his fingers through his hair, feeling the urge to plow his fist into someone's face. His mind pictured Reeder, and it would bring satisfaction to Kurt if he busted up that man's perfect nose and chin, and cut his lips, and gave him a black eye or two.

The bar wasn't very full tonight, but the waitress and the bartender were flirting at the counter. The girl's giggles nearly drowned out the country singer's voice booming from the overhead speakers as he sang about losing his love, his dog, and his truck, and not in that order.

Thankfully, Kurt still had his dog, and his truck, however, he never really had a true love. Strange, but for the past year, he hadn't dated that much, either. He thought it was because he was focusing on his job. But now he realized it was because of Talia. The women he'd gone out with weren't as adorable as Talia Russell. They couldn't make him laugh like she could. They couldn't make him feel like a man, as Talia could. He could be himself around her, but when he was with those other women, he felt as if they wanted more out of him.

Closing his eyes, he tried to get the images of Talia out of his head from the other day when she was wearing that sexy red dress. He couldn't remember a time when he'd seen her so beautiful. She was a lovely woman, however, when Talia was all dolled up like that… she made him breathless.

What he wouldn't give for one moment with her, to take her in his arms, and to kiss her passionately, just to see what it would be like. Yet, every time the thought crossed his mind, he pushed it away. They made great partners. They could practically read each other's minds. Did he really want a girlfriend like that?

Most definitely!

In the year they'd been partnered together, he couldn't think of a time when he'd felt this much jealousy. He hated this emotion, but he didn't know how to make it leave.

From over the strong aroma of the beer, another scent touched his senses. Lilacs… like Talia's perfume.

Quickly, he snapped out of his thoughts and swung around. Talia stood by his side with her arms folded over her bosom as she tapped her toe. Her irritated expression told him she expected an explanation soon.

He motioned to the empty chair. "Want to join me?"

"Not here."

"Where?"

She sighed heavily. "In the car. Now!"

Without waiting for his answer, she turned and marched out of the bar, heading toward the double glass doors of the hotel. He fished in his pocket for the tip, slapped it on the table, and hurried out of the bar. By the time he reached her, she was climbing in her car. He moved around to the passenger side and climbed inside.

The clock on her car's radio read 11:30 pm. He cursed under his breath. She'd been with the perp for four and a half hours?

"Let's get one thing clear," she said with an edge to her voice. "When you're in my ear, you need to stop trying to carry on a conversation with me." She finally turned her head to look at him. Her gaze pierced right through him. "Your main purpose is to take notes. I'm assuming you were recording it, right?"

"Yes. I was recording it."

She released a heavy breath and her shoulders relaxed. "Kurt, do you realize how hard it is to carry on a conversation with someone when someone else is in your ear trying to talk, as well?" She shook her head. "It's hard to focus. It's hard to think, and I really needed to think of what to say to Austin without blowing my cover. We still don't know if he has an alibi for Sunday morning."

He toyed with the gearshift on the console between the bucket seats. His head swam from the alcohol he'd consumed tonight. How many bottles of beer had it been? Two? Four? In four and a half hours, it could have been much more than that. The sports station on the TV inside the bar, and the popcorn, just hadn't satisfied him.

"So what happened after the arm wrestle?" He raised his gaze to her. "Your voices were muffled, and I couldn't hear what you were saying. The only thing I heard," his voice turned harsh, "was when you two laughed."

He studied her face, and when crimson spread across her face, he fisted his hands. They had kissed! She didn't have to tell him. Her expression said it all.

"I'm sorry for losing my earpiece. While we were arm wrestling, Austin started tickling me, and well, I fell to the floor. That's when my earpiece fell out. I quickly grabbed it before he noticed. I didn't dare place it back in my ear and risk him seeing, so I stuffed it in my pants pocket."

He nodded. "I figured as much." Leaning closer to her, he took her hand. "But now you have to understand something. We are partners. We are in this together. We are supposed to watch each other's backs, so if you don't let me in your ear, what good am I going to be?"

She sighed. "Kurt, all I'm asking is that you not try to carry on a conversation with me while I'm trying to talk to someone else. I get distracted so easily, and I can't think of what I'm going to say."

He glanced down at her hand, so very delicate and soft. He stroked his thumb across her knuckles. Would the rest of her arm feel this soft? When she slowly pulled away from him, his chest clenched. It was because of Reeder, he just knew it.

"I better go," he said, turning toward the door.

She grabbed his arm. "You're not going anywhere, Hamill."

Hope sprang inside of him, and he swung his head toward her. But her expression wasn't exactly a pleasant one. She appeared stern. Even her grasp was a little tight. "I'm not?"

"No. You're drunk, so I'm taking you home." Her face relaxed slightly. "After all, I got your back, remember?"

Chuckling, he rested against the seat and nodded. "Then take me home, partner."

They didn't talk much on the way to his apartment. Her radio was playing classic rock, but for some reason, it calmed him. He preferred country music, but it was enjoyable watching Talia drive and sing along with the artists. A few times, she tried to be funny on purpose, and he laughed.

Seeing her this way made him realize she was different on the job. She was more serious and focused. Off duty, she was laid back and easy going. And yes, even silly. His heart couldn't help but squeeze tighter with longing. Why was he allowing his emotions to come forth now when he'd kept them in check for a year? Was it because of his jealousy for Reeder?

No matter what, he needed to find evidence that proved Reeder was the murderer. That was the only way to bring Talia back to him where she belonged.

Finally, she pulled in front of his apartment building and put the car in park. She smiled at him – a smile that had always softened his heart.

"Do I need to walk you to your apartment? Or can you do that yourself?"

"I think I can handle it." He took her hand again. "Thanks for caring enough to want to see me home safe."

"Kurt, I just can't believe you were drinking while on the job. That's not like you at all."

"Yah, I know."

"So why were you? You've hung out in bars before working undercover, and you've never drank. So why now?"

He shrugged. "Maybe it was because I was bored with watching the sports station that was on the TV. Or maybe it was because I was tired of hearing the waitress flirt with the bartender. Then again, I think it was because," he sat up and leaned toward her, "I was tired of hearing my partner play kissy-face with the perp."

She scolded. "Kurt Hamill! I did not play kissy-face with Austin. I'll admit, he did try to kiss me after dinner, but once I started arm wrestling with him, that moment passed."

"Don't tell me he didn't try to kiss you goodnight before you left."

She arched an eyebrow. "Even if he did, it's none of your business."

"I think differently, Russell." He leaned a little closer. "I'm your partner, and you're a police detective. Kissing a perp is wrong on so many different levels, and you know it."

Scowling, she shook her head. "You're full of it, Hamill. Why is it wrong for me to pretend while I'm undercover, and yet it's not wrong for you to do it?" She paused, leaning closer into him. "Many times when you have gone undercover, you have pretended to seduce women just to get answers. What's the difference between what you have done and what I'm doing? Not only that, I've gone undercover before and pretended to seduce a perp for answers, and it never bothered you then."

"Do you mean to tell me you don't know this?" He raised his voice.

"No, Hamill. Please enlighten me."

"I'll tell you what the difference is. The difference is back then, I was never jealous of the perp… not like I am with Reeder." She sucked in a quick breath as her eyes widened, so he quickly continued while he still had the courage. "And another difference is that when you kiss him, you enjoy it, whereas you've never done that before."

She slowly mouthed the word no. His fuzzy mind told him to continue. "And, another difference is that with this case, more than the others, I've been thinking about you differently. I've been wondering what it would be like to be Reeder – to hold you, and kiss you passionately."

"No, Kurt," she whispered.

His breathing was ragged as he stared into her lovely eyes. She didn't pull away, but he didn't think that meant she realized she wanted him as much as he wanted her, either. His confession had probably shocked her, which was only a natural reaction.

Why was he even trying? It was obvious where her heart lied, and it was certainly not with him.

"Oh, never mind. Forget I said anything," he snapped and hurried out of the car.

He focused on the pathway to his apartment. His head pounded with adrenaline, and he cursed his drunkenness. If he'd been sober, he wouldn't have said anything to her. He would have continued to hold the anguish inside. He would have dealt with it, just as he had to deal with this feeling for her ever since they were partnered together.

A couple of times he stumbled up the stairs, but he finally reached his apartment. He fumbled with the keys and tried to get them in the right keyhole, since he could see two of them. Cursing again, he slammed his fist against the door.

"Kurt Hamill! For goodness sake, will you stop?" Talia grabbed his arm and pulled him away from the door. "What are you doing?"

"I'm trying to get in my apartment. What does it look like I'm doing?"

She rolled her eyes. "It looks like you're trying to break into your neighbor's apartment, instead."

She looked back at the door he'd just tried to enter. His fifty-year-old neighbor peeked out, his face white with worry. Talia forced a laugh. "Please forgive Kurt. He's been drinking." Mr. Kirkpatrick nodded and closed the door. Talia looked back at him and held out her hand. "Give me the keys."

If he wasn't so sloshed, maybe he'd feel embarrassed. He was sure it would come tomorrow, along with a huge headache, of course. He gave her the keys and she opened his door. Walking ahead of her, he wearily stepped inside.

As he made his way to the couch, he glanced over his shoulder as she was shutting the door. "Why are you still here?" He practically fell on the piece of furniture.

"Because our conversation is not over." She sat beside him, staring deep into his eyes.

"Actually, it is. Tomorrow, all of this will have just been a nightmare for me."

"Kurt." She grasped his arms. "Do you really feel that way about me, or is that just the alcohol talking?"

He must have heard wrong, because he could have sworn her voice was softer. He blinked several times, trying to make his vision clear. Why was she looking at him with so much tenderness in her eyes?

"I really feel that way. The alcohol is helping me to get it off my chest, since it's been there since you first entered our precinct."

"Why haven't you said anything before now?"

"Because I didn't realize it until we became partners, and by then, it was too late."

Smiling, she lay back against the couch, keeping her gaze on him. "The truth is, I had those feeling for you, too. I didn't want to say anything because I enjoyed being your partner. I didn't want to ruin that."

The alcohol must be disturbing his hearing, because he for sure didn't hear her correctly. "You... you were in love with me?"

Shyly, she shrugged. "I don't know if what I felt was love, but I definitely had a crush on you."

He turned toward her and pulled her in his arms. "Had? Are you saying you don't feel that way about me now?"

Talia's expression wavered, and he wasn't sure if she was sad or scared. Maybe both. She also appeared hesitant to answer.

"Kurt, I... don't know."

"Shh, don't say that," he whispered as he lowered his mouth to hers. She didn't pull away, but allowed him to kiss her. The kiss was soft, and sweet. *Sweet?* No, he didn't want sweet. As he opened his mouth to deepen the kiss, she pushed him away.

"Kurt, this isn't right."

"Yes, it is. I can make it right." He tried to bring her back, but she rose from the couch, shaking her head.

"Kurt, when I kiss you, I don't want to taste alcohol. Sorry, but it's not the right time to kiss you."

Relief flooded through him, knowing it was just the beer that repelled her. "All right. Then, um... I'll see you tomorrow?"

She smiled at him before moving to the door. "Well, if you can see through that headache, sure, I'll see you tomorrow at work."

He chuckled and relaxed into the couch as she walked out and shut the door. His heart soared with happiness. Perhaps there was a chance to make Talia love him for more than a partner.

ELEVEN

Talia's headache was probably just as bad as she figured Kurt's would be today. But for different reasons, of course.

She hesitated before walking into the police station. Her emotions were all over the place. When she'd left Kurt's place last night, she was floating on air. She couldn't believe he would feel the same way about her, and yet now it almost seemed like it was too late. Did she still have feelings for him, or were they being blocked because of her attraction to Austin Reeder?

Frowning, she rubbed her forehead. When she'd kissed Kurt last night, the strong beer taste in his mouth turned her off. For a brief moment before she was disgusted by that, an image of Austin popped into her head.

She hadn't lied to Kurt about what she and Austin had done after she took out her earpiece. She'd actually enjoyed herself with him. They laughed. They talked about anything, and she was finally starting to feel like she was on a real date. When he walked her to the elevator, he did kiss her. It was very brief, but oh, so memorable.

Proceeding into the building, she held herself strong. She and Kurt needed to talk about last night. Things would be awkward between them if they didn't. When she reached the section of the building that held her precinct, her attention zoomed toward Kurt's desk. Empty. He wouldn't have called in sick. He'd had hangover headaches before and still showed up to work the next day. Maybe he was embarrassed about admitting his feelings.

Groaning, she rubbed her forehead again. Now she felt like an idiot. Why had she told him about her infatuation? She should have known he'd been drinking too much, and he wasn't thinking straight—

"Russell?"

She froze when she heard the harsh tone of Sergeant Feakes' voice. Slowly, she turned to look in the man's direction.

He was a powerfully tall man, but in his mid-forties, he still had a full head of curly black hair without a hint of gray.

"Yes, sir," she answered.

"I need to speak with you and Hamill ASAP." His gaze moved around the room. "Where is he?"

"Um, I don't know sir. I'm sure he'll be in at any moment."

He threw her a glare and pointed to the conference room. "I want you both in there as soon as he shows his face. Understood?"

"Yes, sir."

Talia wished she knew why he was always snapping at her. What had she done to make him mad? She would think it had something to do with her recent undercover case with Austin, but the sergeant had acted that way with her since she first met him.

She wandered back toward the front door. Still no sign of Kurt. Then she moved to the window and peered outside. Kurt's Honda Accord slowly pulled into a parking place. When he exited the car, he held a cup – probably black coffee, no sugar, no cream, just the way he liked it – and took careful steps toward the building.

Biting her lip, she tried not to laugh. Although she had a headache, too, at least it wasn't breaking her skull with every step, and threatening to bring everything in her stomach up, like she knew his hangover was doing. She hoped the sergeant would be nicer to Kurt, instead of being harsh as he'd been with her.

When Kurt finally made his appearance, she walked toward him. His narrowed gaze stayed on her until she stopped in front of him.

"For some reason, Sergeant Feakes looks like he's on the warpath. He wants us both in the conference room, immediately."

Kurt cussed. "I hope my headache can withstand it."

"So do I."

Side-by-side she walked with Kurt into the conference room. When she noticed the others in the precinct, she breathed a sigh of relief. Thank goodness it wasn't just her and Kurt the sergeant wanted to speak with.

Once she and Kurt took their seats, Sergeant Feakes did his customary pacing in front of everyone. By now, she was used to this. She assumed it was the man's way of trying to get his point across. Sometimes it worked, but most of the time it didn't.

"The mayor wants answers. Kalama Kane's case is stretching into a week, and that's too long." He glared at Tyrone and Gibbs. "What have you found out?"

Henry Gibbs certainly didn't fit the part of a police detective. The blond man's clean-cut shaven face, and his classy threads, made him look like someone who took modeling seriously. If he had any muscles like Kurt, she'd be surprised. Now she wondered if his fingernails were manicured, too.

As Gibbs started explaining who he'd questioned and what they found, she moved her gaze to Kurt. His attention wasn't on the sergeant or the other two detectives, but it was on her. When she met his stare, he quickly looked away. Her heart fluttered, but it wasn't quite like the fluttering it did whenever Austin looked at her, or touched her, or kissed her.

"Russell and Hamill?" Sergeant Feakes' voice rose higher. "You've had enough time to question Mr. Reeder. What's going on with him?"

She glanced at Kurt to see if he was going to speak, but by the grimace on his expression as he squeezed his eyes closed, she realized he probably wouldn't talk yet.

"Sergeant, as you know, I went undercover wearing an earpiece. I met with the perp last night. Kurt was able to get most of the conversation recorded. But during my evening with Reeder, I was led to believe he wasn't involved with Kalama Kane. He mentioned helping her get out of a sticky situation when she worked for Belle's Escort Service. Kurt and I wondered if this was a call girl service." The other men snickered behind their hands. She rolled her eyes and continued. "But Reeder admits to giving Kalama money, but when she wanted more and he turned her down, they parted ways, and he claims he'd not seen her since then."

Feakes paused and glanced at the others. "Have any of you heard of Belle's Escort Service?"

Negative mumbling circled the group

"Russell and Hamill, I want you to follow up on this lead."

"Yes, sir," Kurt muttered.

Feakes cocked his head as he peered directly at Talia. "So are we taking him off the suspect's list?"

"Yes, I think—"

"No, not yet," Kurt interrupted.

She gasped and glared at him. What was he doing? After he had listened in on their conversation last night, why wasn't he convinced as she was?

"Explain yourself," Feakes snapped.

Kurt inhaled deeply and sat up straighter. "Because Reeder kept in touch with Kalama, and even gave her money to set up her own business – which he admits to not knowing what it was – Reeder had mentioned that they argued and she stormed out."

"Seriously?" Talia shook her head, not believing Kurt. "That's why you think he's still a suspect?"

"Yes." He met her glare. "Because he had upset her. And he even mentioned that she threatened him before leaving."

"But nothing was done about it. Reeder hadn't seen her since that day."

"And how do we know he's not lying," Kurt spoke slower. "Because she threatened him, that would give her more reason to see it through by blackmailing him. And he's not going to admit being blackmailed, especially because the woman is dead, which he's smart enough to know that makes him a suspect."

Talia gnashed her teeth. She wanted to shake some sense into Kurt, regardless of his headache.

"Hamill's right." Feakes gave a sharp nod. "Reeder stays on the list." He moved his attention to the others, beginning to ask them the same question.

Talia tried to communicate her frustration toward Kurt through her eyes, but he wouldn't look at her for very long. Finally, she bumped against him with her arm.

"Give it up, Russell," he whispered. "You know I'm right."

"Actually, you're so very wrong." She kept her voice low, too.

"We'll talk about this later."

"Yes, we will." She folded her arms across her chest and focused on Sergeant Feakes. Too bad she couldn't hear a word he was saying, because her mind was putting arguments together for when she and Kurt were alone. Once she released her frustrations, he was going to wish he stayed home.

As soon as the briefing was adjourned, she followed Kurt out. He reached his office, and nearly collapsed on his chair. Resting his elbows on his desk, he laid his head in his hands.

"Kurt, we need to talk," she said, sitting on the empty chair by his desk.

"Not now we don't."

She huffed and glared his way, even though he didn't care enough to look at her and see it. "I mean it, Hamill."

"Talia, while I'm trying to recover from my headache," he muttered into his hands, "why don't you go to your own desk and start researching Belle's Escort Service. Didn't you hear Feakes? We need to interview them."

She grumbled under her breath and marched to her desk. At this moment, she was so mad at Kurt, she could... could... Well, she wasn't quite sure what she would do to him, but one thing was for sure, it wouldn't be pleasant.

How dare he not believe Austin was innocent? Although a few questions still lingered in her mind, for the most part, she didn't think he could do it. She'd gotten to know him a little better last night, and he was sweet and caring. Good grief, he was going to actually give her money to help her with rent just so she wouldn't get evicted, and yet, he hadn't even known her that well. She hadn't met anyone with a bigger heart.

She glanced up to see Willy Tyrone giving her a leery stare. This was a man that most people didn't want to mess with. He was nice looking for a body builder. He never admitted that's what he did off work hours, but how else would he get his body so buff, unless he took steroids, which she seriously doubted. Two weeks ago, she'd teased him for shaving his head, but now, she rather liked seeing his bald head every day.

She wished he'd stop looking at her as if she'd done something wrong. Obviously, he was taking Kurt's side in everything.

As she typed the name of the escort service into the computer, her hard keystrokes echoed in the office. Yes, she was upset, and she wanted everyone to know it, especially Kurt. Several listings popped up on the monitor, and yet none of them were in Honolulu.

She drummed her fingers on the desk, trying to think of something else she could do to find Belle's business, but the only thing going through her mind was Kurt. He was as hardheaded as she was, so how could she convince him Austin should not be a suspect?

Casually, she glanced his way. He was still nursing his hangover headache. He held his Starbucks cup of coffee close and sipped it from time to time. She didn't feel sorry for him one bit. Not now!

The buzz from her cell phone jerked her out of her angry thoughts and she withdrew the cell from her pocket. When she read who had just sent her a text, her heartbeat quickened with excitement.

I hope you're having a wonderful day. I'm not, because I'm constantly thinking about you. When can I see you again? Tonight?

Perhaps she shouldn't have given Austin her cell number, but she'd had such an incredible evening with him. Because she'd felt he had done nothing wrong, she went against the rules and gave him her number. She just prayed Feakes never got wind of it. Or Kurt, for that matter.

She smiled wide and texted him back. *I've been thinking about you, too. I'm free tonight. Are you?*

Within seconds, he sent back a reply. *I'll cancel all my appointments. Nothing will keep me from seeing you.*

Butterflies danced inside her chest, making her feel giddy all over. She didn't know what to say to him now, but he sent another text only moments later.

Can I come pick you up this time and make it a real date?

Her heart dropped. No. She couldn't allow that. What if he wanted to come inside her apartment? What if he noticed some of the awards she'd received from being on the task force or those she'd been given while attending the police academy? It wasn't time to tell him the truth about her identity. *No, not yet. I'm not ready for you to see where I live.*

Talia, I'll need to know eventually, especially if I need to give your landlord the money to pay your rent. Besides that, I have another surprise for you.

Groaning, she slunk in her chair. The web of deceit she had begun was growing, and she wanted it to stop. Perhaps she could hide the trophies and awards, and she could also talk to her landlord and explain things about the rent.

She slowly blew out a heavy breath. *Let's meet somewhere first, and then I'll take you back to my apartment.* After she'd typed it, she gasped. What if he took it the wrong way? Hopefully, he wouldn't think… Oh, dear. This couldn't be good.

He texted back with a smiley face. *For drinks, maybe?*

Her heart skipped a beat. *Yes. Drinks.*

What time? he texted.

Seven.

Where?

She paused in thought. They'd have to go someplace that wasn't private, but then also, someplace where nobody would recognize her. Her mind scrambled for out of the way places. *Kaka'ako Waterfront Park.*

Yes. It's the perfect spot for romance. The beach is very pretty at night with the moonlight reflecting on the clear ocean water.

How could she have forgotten about that? Well, it was too late to say something else. And really, they were out in the open. What would it hurt?

I'll see you then. Let's meet in front of the Ala Moana Apartments. I can't wait!

She smiled and tucked her cell back in her pocket. She couldn't wait, either.

As she glanced around the room, she noticed Kurt again. This time, he was watching her. His expression dripped with sadness, and her gut clenched. He couldn't possibly know who she'd been texting. And yet, if she'd been smiling wide the whole time, Kurt would know.

Trying to ignore his heart-wrenching sad, puppy-dog eyes, she turned back to her computer in hopes of doing more searching for the escort service. Even if she didn't find anything, she still would pretend to be working. Although she wanted to talk with Kurt, right now was not a good time. She didn't want anything to ruin her happy mood.

TWEVLE

Austin paced in front of Ala Moana Apartments while waiting for Talia. Although it wasn't seven o'clock yet, he was anxious. Perhaps overly so. He glanced across the way, toward the beach. Palm trees lined the main roads, and tonight their leaves swayed gently in the breeze. There was an exact spot to stand that would allow one to look across the water and see all the colors of the sunset reflected in the ocean. At this time of night, the sun was just in the right spot, and created such a romantic sunset.

Of course, he'd been too busy these past few years, building up his assets and striving to reach the billionaire status, to take a night off just to enjoy the lovely view. He still didn't know what it was about Talia that made him want to take a break from life and just enjoy a woman's company, but he was anxious to do this with her.

His cell buzzed, and he held his breath, hoping it wasn't Talia canceling their date. Thankfully, it was his friend. "Hey, Ariki."

"I hope I'm not bothering you."

"No. I'm just waiting to meet a woman at the beach. Why? What's up?"

"Wh-what? You are meeting a woman – on your *own*? That doesn't sound like the Austin Reeder I know."

Austin laughed. "No, it doesn't, but that's all right. I felt I was stuck in a rut, and I needed a change."

"Well, I'm glad to hear it. I was actually calling about that one woman you asked me about the other day."

"Talia?"

"Yes, that one."

"Have you found out anything about her?"

"No. That's why I'm calling. To let you know that everything I've tried is a dead end."

Austin grinned. "Well, my friend, luck is on my side, because she came back."

"She did?"

"Yes, and that's who I'm meeting tonight."

"Did she tell you how she knows me?"

Austin shook his head and chuckled. "Yes. She told me the whole story." As he explained it to his friend, his smile continued to widen. Images of Talia floated through his mind, making him more anxious. Her beauty was intoxicating, and he wanted to sample her passionate kisses once more. But it was more than that. Last night, he wasn't a billionaire, and she wasn't a woman desperate for money. They were two lonely souls enjoying the evening together. She made him laugh, and that pleased him almost as much as her passionate kisses.

"She's a friend of Kalama's?" Ariki's voice wavered.

"I guess. But Kalama was the one who recommended me."

"Hmm… That doesn't sound right. I didn't know Kalama had women friends."

Austin shrugged. "Apparently, she does."

"Do you think Talia is lying?"

"Why would she lie?" Austin shook his head. "She was a distressed woman, and that's exactly how she acted that first afternoon in my suite. No, I don't think she's lying."

"So, you're really going to help her?"

"Of course."

Ariki tsked on the other end of the phone. "My friend, you have always been the kind of guy who helps abandoned animals. I suppose you'll always be that way."

Tilting back his head, Austin belted out a laugh. "I suppose you were being polite just then, right? So why did I take it as an insult?"

"Take it however you want it. I've always known you to help the underdog."

"Okay, I'll take it as a compliment."

"Well, I'll hang up now and let you enjoy your evening. Let me know if you need me to set you up with another woman."

Austin relaxed and looked back up the street, hoping to see Talia's car. "No, I think I'll be fine for a while."

"Good. Don't let her take advantage of you."

Ariki hung up before Austin could reply to his friend's remark. Why would Talia take advantage of him? Was it because he offered her money? He'd known people who'd used him to get to his money, but Talia wasn't like that. Even when she thought about being a call girl, at least in her mind, she was working for the money.

So what if Austin liked to help stray animals? Women like Talia just shouldn't do that for a living. She had too much going for her, and he wouldn't let her give up her morals just because she was desperate.

"Excuse me, sir. Can you tell me where the Ala Moana Apartments are?"

He turned to look at the sweet voice coming from behind him. Talia stood with her fingers tucked into the front pocket of her tight jeans, rocking back and forth on the heels of her running shoes. She wore a slightly baggy purple blouse that buttoned down the front and had a small collar. Hanging over her shoulder was a black leather purse. Her hair was pulled back in a ponytail. He wasn't sure he liked that. He enjoyed her casual appearance tonight, but he wanted her hair long and flowing over her shoulders, which gave her that sensual look.

"Sorry, I didn't see you," he said.

"I guess I'm pretty good at sneaking up on people."

He ran his gaze over her again, feeling almost overdressed. He wore his jeans and athletic shoes, but his shirt was a lot dressier than hers.

Austin held out his hand. "Well, shall we stroll down the waterfront?"

She slipped her palm against his and entwined her fingers with his. "I can't think of anything I'd like better at the moment."

"Me, neither."

"How was your day?" she asked. "If I remember correctly, you were supposed to be taking over a new hotel today. Right?"

He squeezed her hand gently. "You have a good memory. Yes, that was today, and the takeover went smoothly. I'm now the proud owner of the Sheridan Hotel."

"Congratulations."

"And that," he continued quickly, "brings me to the surprise I have for you."

Her gaze stayed on him. He liked how she trusted he wouldn't lead them into any trees, instead of watching where she was walking.

"It does? What surprise?" She narrowed her eyes on him, suspiciously.

"You'd mentioned yesterday that you were out of a job. Well, I'm wondering what kind of experience you have in clerical work."

"Um…a little. Why?"

Her expression still appeared skeptical, so he wouldn't tease her any longer. "Because I'll need someone to manage the bookkeeping at the Sheridan. I was hoping you could do that job. I'll pay you well." Her jaw dropped and her eyes widened, so he quickly continued, "And, I was thinking, if you need a new place to live, you could live in the penthouse suite in the Sheridan. I plan on renovating those rooms immediately, so the place will be available by the end of the month."

She opened her mouth to speak, then closed it, and then opened it again, but still no words came out. Finally, she gave him a grateful smile as tears spiked in her amazing rusty eyes.

"You'd really do that for me?" she asked in a shaky voice.

"I would." He stopped and faced her, taking both of her hands in his. "Last night, you proved to me what a fun and exciting woman you are. You're intelligent, and beautiful, and I've never met anyone like you. I don't give jobs and homes to just anyone, you know. I happen to think you're an amazing woman." He winked.

"I've never met anyone like you, either, Austin. You are so giving, and you have such a huge heart. What kind of guy helps people in need anymore, without wanting something in return?" She paused. "Um… do you want something in return?"

"Actually, yes." He gathered her in his arms. "I'm hoping in exchange for what I'm offering, that you will continue to be my friend and make me laugh."

One side of her mouth lifted higher than the other. "What if I only want to be friends? After all, it's not right to date my boss."

He'd not really thought of that, but then, it wasn't fair of him to expect more. Then she'd be nothing more than a high priced mistress, and he didn't want her to get that kind of reputation.

Chuckling, he kissed her on the forehead. "Then I'll tell you what we can do. What if we date before you take the job, and after you start work we'll see what happens in our relationship? If we're only meant to be friends, I'll accept that."

"You're pretty amazing yourself, you know." She leaned against him and looked up into his face. "But I think that's a good idea. We'll date, but then pull back once I start working for you."

He smiled wide. "So you'll accept the position?"

"How can I turn it down? It'll be perfect for me."

"And the penthouse suite? Will you take that?"

"Well, it's probably more expensive than my one-bedroom apartment, so maybe I should just stay there. After all, once I get a job, I'll be able to make rent every month."

He stroked her cheek. "You are certainly a hard woman to figure out. Most women I know would have jumped at the chance to live in the penthouse suite."

She shrugged. "It's like you said – I'm not like most women."

His heart melted. It had been doing that a lot since meeting her. He dropped his gaze to her mouth. It really wasn't the time to kiss her, and yet, he just couldn't resist. Not now. Not after realizing that she really wasn't after his money. He would have known if she had accepted the suite with the job.

"No," he said in a deep voice, "you're not like the others, which is why I can't stop thinking about you." He swept his lips over hers, and she sighed, relaxing into his embrace. When he finally covered his mouth over hers, she didn't pull away. Instead, she met his soft kisses, and even when he gradually deepened the kiss, she still responded the way he'd hoped she would.

Her arms were around his waist, and she moved her hands over his back in small circles. His body burned wherever she touched. Although he'd been with many women, none of them excited him the way Talia was doing now. None of them kissed this good, either. And especially, none of them made his heart melt. The strong burning in his chest was not heartburn, but for sure, his heart was involved with this particular emotion.

Did he believe in love at first sight? No, however, Talia was certainly making him think differently.

Suddenly, he felt her jerk in his arms. Then he heard the slapping of shoes on the pavement as someone started running. Talia swung around toward the man running away from them. In the stranger's hand, he carried her purse.

She cursed and darted after the mugger. Finally, Austin's hazy mind cleared, and he realized someone was stealing her purse. He muttered a curse and ran after them. Talia yelled at the man, but of course, the mugger didn't stop.

It surprised Austin how fast she was. Of course, the first time he met her, he thought she worked out a lot, but seeing her in action, proved that she was definitely fit. In fact, she was gaining on the purse-snatcher.

Just inches away from the man, Talia lunged and landed on him. They fell on the ground at the base of a palm tree, and she maneuvered herself on top of the thief. The man beneath her struggled and appeared as if he would knock Talia off him and get away. Seconds later, she punched him in the face, which calmed the man considerably.

Once Austin reached them, he stopped. His breaths were coming fast and heavy, reminding him that he needed to start exercising regularly. To have this slip of a woman outrun him was quite humiliating.

She held down the man's arms. "Austin, call 911."

He fumbled with his phone, still amazed of what he'd just witnessed. As he gave the emergency operator their location, he watched as Talia expertly handled the thief.

Austin quickly pocketed his cell, and moved closer to her. "Talia? Let me take over. I'll keep him still."

"No, I'm good," she told him over her shoulder.

Surprisingly enough, she appeared to be handling it well. Her hands were holding the man's arms, and the way she placed her knees on him, made Austin realize this woman knew what she was doing.

"Austin?"

"Yes." He stepped closer, still feeling out of place.

"Will you take my purse from him?"

"Sure." Austin bent and pulled her purse out of the man's hand.

The thief's nose was bleeding, and his eye was beginning to swell. He shot daggers at Talia and muttered cuss words.

Time seemed to go quickly once the police arrived. They took down Talia's and Austin's information on what happened as they cuffed the guy and threw him into the back seat of the squad car.

When the police drove off, Talia bent and wiped off the dirt from her knees. Austin was still at a loss for words, and yet, he wanted to know more. As she rose, he circled his arms around her and gazed deeply into her eyes.

"Are you all right?"

She hiccuped a laugh. "Of course I am." She caressed his trimmed beard. "Are you?"

"My sweet woman, I'm not the one who that man attacked, nor was I the one who chased after him."

"I know, but… well, I'm still worried about you." She trailed her fingers along his cheekbone. "You sort of lost color in your face."

"Yeah, because I was scared to death you'd get hurt."

She shook her head. "So you're probably wondering why I didn't get hurt, right?"

He nodded.

"Well, a few years ago, I took self-defense classes. When I felt that man snatch my purse, I didn't think twice in running after him."

"Yes, you ran after him quite well."

She laughed. "I love running."

"I can tell. I can also tell you love taking down the bad guys."

Her eyes widened, but within seconds she nodded. "You're right. I do."

He gathered her closer and kissed her moist forehead. "My hero."

She laughed again and tilted her head back to look into his eyes. "Now that's something I've never been called before."

"I don't know why. If you go around stopping crimes from happening, you should be called a hero."

She bit her bottom lip as her gaze combed over his face slowly. "Do you… um, I mean, would you like a woman who goes around stopping crimes?"

"I never thought of it, but I suppose I would like it, especially if that woman was you."

She heaved a breath and pulled out of his arms. She took her purse and slowly unzipped it. "Austin, there's something I need to tell you."

He wasn't sure he liked her expression. It wavered between sadness and guilt. His heart dropped. He didn't think he wanted to hear what she had to say now.

THIRTEEN

Talia couldn't lie to him anymore. Deep in her heart she knew he hadn't murdered Kalama Kane. Just because he'd had dealings with her, didn't make him the criminal. In her mind, he was off her suspects' list. Kurt would hate her, but she had to go with her gut feeling, and right now, it was telling her to trust Austin.

She took his hand and led him to the park bench, sitting down first with him next to her. The unease in his gaze worried her. He'd be upset, but she hoped he would understand and forgive her.

"Austin, I think we need to talk about something that's really important." She stroked her hand slowly across his chest, loving the way his muscles flexed. As she prepared her thoughts carefully, her cell buzzed.

Inwardly, she groaned. It was probably work. For once she'd like to have an evening all to herself, or to be on a date without having it ruined.

She pulled out her cell and read the text from Kurt. *The autopsy report just came in. Meet me there in fifteen.*

Frowning, she slid the phone back into the pocket of her jeans. Kalama Kane's autopsy report was important. This would show the detectives exactly what was used to kill the woman. Unfortunately, her talk with Austin must be postponed.

"Bad news?" he asked after a few moments of silence.

"Yes and no." She released a heavy breath and managed a sympathetic smile. "It kills me that I need to end our date, but I do." She leaned in and kissed his cheek. She wanted to do more, but if their mouths met together in a passionate kiss now, she'd never meet Kurt on time. "Can I get a raincheck on our date?"

Austin nodded. "Anytime you want." He stood and took her hand. "I'll walk you back to your car."

"Ah, my hero." She winked.

He laughed and wrapped one arm around her shoulders as they headed back to her car. "Tomorrow, I'm going to be at the Sheridan Hotel most of the day, but if you want to come by to see me, and let me show you around, please drop by and surprise me."

She nodded. "I think I will."

"Do you know where it is?"

"If I remember correctly, isn't it downtown?"

"Yes, it is." He kissed her forehead.

She sighed and wrapped her arms around his waist as they walked. Being with him like this was so cozy. She never wanted it to end. But back in the dark recesses of her mind, she also knew this wasn't a fairy-tale, even if she wanted Austin to be her Prince Charming.

When they stopped at her car, he cupped her face to give her another kiss, but she kept it short and sweet. Because of the way her whole body melted whenever they were together, she knew if she participated fully in the kiss, she would want to stay in his arms all night.

"I'll call you or drop by the hotel tomorrow," she said as she climbed into her car.

He stood and watched her drive away. His energetic smile would be etched in her memory forever.

When she reached the crime lab, Kurt was just climbing out of his vehicle. He waited until she was parked before he opened the door for her.

"Hi," he said in a tight voice.

"Hi," she replied. "Thanks for texting me and letting me know. I'm anxious to hear what Conover has found."

Kurt nodded. "Conover has been very precise in a lot of his findings. I trust him fully."

"I agree." She hurried up the stairs and into the building with Kurt following.

She hoped he wouldn't ask about her evening. She didn't want to lie to him. They still hadn't talked about their kiss or their confessions the other night. But more than that, she wanted to discuss the reasoning behind his thoughts to why

Austin should still be considered a suspect, especially, when she thought completely opposite. Maybe she'd try to get him to talk to her tonight about everything. He didn't smell as if he'd consumed a whole barrel of beer this time.

They walked into the medical examiner's room, and Conover stood over the body. Sergeant Feakes was here, along with Tyrone, but the others were absent.

Conover moved to the body and withdrew the sheet. Talia hated to see dead bodies that had been opened up to examine. Out of everything, this was the thing she hated most.

"The victim died by a fierce blow to the head." Conover pointed to the injury. "When I examined the skull, however, I found this, embedded inside." He held up a Ziplock bag with a sharp object that was made of steel.

Feakes and Tyrone examined it and then handed it to her and Kurt.

"Do you know where the piece could have come from?" the Sergeant asked.

"I believe so. After running several tests, I think it's from a historic weapon."

Talia shook her head, not believing what she heard. "A historic weapon?"

Nodding, Conover walked over to his desk and picked up a picture of a weapon that she figured was used in medieval times.

"You'd mentioned the victim had a list of names of powerful and wealthy men, correct?" Conover asked, and they all nodded. "If you find the man who has a collection of ancient weapons, you just might find your killer."

Talia and Kurt exchanged glances. She scrambled to remember if Austin's place had such a collection, but she honestly couldn't remember. Besides, why was she even thinking about Austin that way? In her mind, she'd erased him from her suspects' list.

"There was another thing I discovered," Conover continued. "When I ran a toxicology screen, I found traces of poison in her bloodstream. I ran tests on the victim's clothes that were left in the bathroom when she had taken a bath, and they had stains from where she'd vomited. I checked her arms for traces of needles, but there weren't any. I believe the victim had consumed something which had poison in it." He shook his head. "If the blow to the head hadn't killed her, the poison would have."

Kurt cussed. "Apparently, the killer was serious about killing Kalama one way or another." The other men in the room didn't verbally answer, but nodded in agreement.

"Conover," Tyrone asked, "in your testing, could you tell what she had for breakfast that morning?"

Nodding, Conover lifted his notebook and scanned the contents. "Pancakes and bacon with coffee."

Talia tapped her finger on her chin. Now the question was, had she stayed at home to eat or went out?

Feakes cleared his throat. "We need everyone to return to the suspects' homes and see if they have an ancient collection of weapons. Because this was the exact cause of the death, finding the weapon is crucial."

She walked with Kurt outside toward the parking lot in silence. She tried to piece in her mind what could have happened at the crime scene. Kalama must have been with the killer before she'd gone in to take a bath. But, she wouldn't have brought this person back to her parent's home. Instead, Kalama would have met this person somewhere else, had drinks with them, perhaps a late breakfast of pancakes and bacon before returning to her parent's house. The poison would have made her ill, and after regurgitating what was in her stomach, she would have wanted to take a shower to wash it off in hopes of feeling better again.

"Kurt? Has Jasmine pulled the report to see which purchases Kalama used with her credit or debit card?"

He shrugged. "Good question. I'm not sure, but if she hasn't, we'll ask her to do that."

"I'm thinking," Talia continued, "that Kalama probably met the killer for breakfast. Maybe it was there where the killer poisoned her."

"Good thinking." He walked to his car first and pointed at the driver's side. "Why don't we go together and check on some leads."

"Sure." She climbed in and closed the door.

Once Kurt was inside, he started the car and backed out. "Call Jasmine now and ask her."

Talia quickly got on her cell and called the other woman. Thankfully, Jasmine had pulled the report, and she read off the few places Kalama had gone that morning where she used her credit card. When Talia ended the call, she grinned at Kurt. "Looks like we'll be going to Heavenly Island Café."

His smile widened, showing his polished white teeth, which contrasted against his dark brown beard. "Am I to understand Kalama had breakfast there that morning?"

Talia nodded. "And I'm betting money that she met up with a man."

"Me, too." He winked. "Oh, and the next place I want to check out is Isabella's Escort Service."

Confusion filled her and she narrowed her gaze on him. "Isabella's Escort Service? I thought Austin had mentioned a Belle's Escort Service."

"Since there is no business by that name, I'm thinking Belle is a nickname for Isabella."

"Ah, good thinking, partner." She chuckled. "I never suspected Belle would be short for another name." She drummed her fingers on the armrest of the car. "Are there other escort services in Honolulu?"

"A few, but not with a name that would fit with Belle."

It didn't take long before he pulled up in front of the pancake house. Thankfully, they were open for dinner as well as breakfast. Talia and Kurt walked in together. Immediately, they were greeted by the hostess. They both flashed the woman their badges.

"I'm Detective Hamill, and this is my partner, Detective Russell with HPD. Can we speak with the manager?"

The girl looked like she was still in high school with mostly brown hair, but a section was colored in blue, and a lip ring, widened her eyes. She swallowed hard. "Um, the manager doesn't work tonight. But my supervisor is here."

"Please get your supervisor," Talia said.

The girl hurried off, and Talia scoped out the seating area. Tonight, there were only five man/woman couples, one couple that were both female, and one family with four kids, partaking of the restaurant's fine dining. She raised her gaze to the ceiling, looking for any security cameras. "I don't see any more cameras," she whispered.

"Me, either." Kurt moved to the cash register, his attention went everywhere, even on the floor. Then he pointed to a spot on the wall behind the register. "I think that's the security camera."

She stood close to him until their elbows touched. "Yeah, I think it is."

"Can I help you?"

A man, who was in his late twenties, approached them with the blue-haired girl tagging behind. Kurt moved in front of Talia to greet the man.

"We are HPD Detectives, and I need to ask you a few questions about Sunday morning between eight and ten. Were you, or any of your employees, working that morning?"

"I was." The blond man nodded.

Kurt reached into his vest pocket and pulled out a picture. "This woman was having breakfast that morning. Do you remember her?"

The overweight man's gaze narrowed as he studied the picture. Slowly, he nodded. "I think I do. If I remember right, she was waiting for her friend."

"Do you know if her friend ever showed up?" Talia asked, coming closer.

The man scratched his double chin. "Yes."

"By chance," Talia continued, "did you recognize him as someone of importance here in Honolulu?"

The man frowned. "I don't remember thinking that at all."

"Do you think," Kurt added, "that you could describe him?"

The man breathed in slowly, and then exhaled. "All I can remember was that he was a good-looking man. He and the woman looked good together because they were both very well-dressed people. I do remember that they argued about something, and then the man left before the woman."

"Thanks for your help." Kurt pointed to the wall behind the cash register. "One last thing. Is that a security camera?"

"Yes."

Kurt continued. "Are there others?"

"No."

"Could we get Sunday's recording?"

"I, um…" The man scratched his double chin again. "I'll have to get the manager's approval."

"Would you call him right now?" Talia asked. "We could get a search warrant if the manager doesn't comply."

"Yes, ma'am." The overweight man hurried back into the other room.

During the wait, she scanned the occupants, again. One man faced her and kept raising his gaze to her and Kurt. When he caught her looking his way, he quickly lowered his gaze and leaned across the table as if he was talking to the woman sitting across from him.

"What's your theory?" Kurt asked her.

She snapped her attention away from the couple and walked to the bench near the cash register and sat. "I think Kalama met one of the men on her list to try and bribe them into going with her new call girl business. And, just like what happened with Austin, I think this guy rudely refused her and then stormed out of the restaurant."

"What about the poison?" Kurt lifted a leg, resting his foot against the bench, as he met her gaze.

"Well, that gets a little tricky. I suppose she had tried to bribe this man, or even blackmail him before, and he was tired of it. He could have met her here with the poison, ready to pour it in her coffee. Maybe he could have tried to stop her from doing something that she'd threatened to do, and when things didn't go his way, he could have poured the powder in her coffee when she wasn't looking."

"That's plausible." Kurt stroked his trimmed beard, the familiar way he'd always done when he was deep in thought. "I do agree with you that Kalama was trying to blackmail him or threaten him in some way."

"You do?" Strange how he agreed with her now, but he couldn't agree with her about Austin.

"Yes. Kalama had control of the meeting, because if she hadn't, her male friend wouldn't have stormed out of here."

"That's a brilliant theory." She smiled.

"Excuse me," some guy snapped at Kurt as he came to pay for his meal.

Kurt moved away from the cash register and stood on the other side of Talia.

The woman waiting for the man at the register had her head bent as she pretended to dig through her purse. Unless the lady was trying to find the kitchen sink in there, Talia didn't believe the woman looked like she was searching for anything of importance.

The girl with the blue section of hair rang the man up and gave him back his change. The man and the woman rushed past Talia with their heads turned, as if they didn't want her to see them.

Curious, Talia stood and walked to the front door, watching as they scurried to their vehicles. Usually, people only hurried like that unless it was raining. She looked at the license plate, and quickly wrote down the number, and then jotted down the make and model of the car.

"What's up?" Kurt asked behind her.

"I don't know. These two just appeared… suspicious. The way they acted was like they were trying to get out of here as fast as they could. And," she looked over her shoulder at Kurt, "they were desperately trying to keep us from studying their faces."

"How odd."

Talia nodded. "Very odd."

From behind them, someone cleared his throat. She and Kurt turned to see the supervisor again. He wrung his beefy hands against his wide belly.

"The manager says I can show you the video."

As they followed him in the back, Kurt walked beside Talia, but just far enough behind that his hand moved to her waist. She peeked at him over her shoulder and he gave her a wink. Her heart tripped, and her legs nearly followed. What was he doing? Why was he acting so possessive now?

For the next half hour, they watched the video as many people came to the cash register to pay, starting at eight o'clock, and going nearly until ten. Talia hadn't met all of the suspects, but pictures of these men were added to the board in the detective's room. So far, nobody looked suspicious.

She sat at the desk as Kurt stood behind her, leaning over her shoulder. The cologne that she'd always loved smelling on him, filled the air around her, creating comfort inside of her. Strange to think she'd always felt this way when he was near, as if nothing bad could ever happen to her because he was her protector.

She mentally shook off the silly fantasy she'd had since becoming his partner of them falling in love, and focused on the recording. So far, she didn't notice anyone. As they watched one man pay for his meal, behind him another man rushed by, bumping into him on his way.

"Stop it right there," Kurt snapped, pointing to the screen. The supervisor followed his instructions. "Rewind it, and play it really slow."

As they watched it again, Talia paid closer attention to the man in the background. She could only see the side of his face, but it was still quite blurred. The man wore a black leather jacket. By his movements, it was obvious, he was very upset.

"Play it back again," Kurt ordered.

The supervisor did as asked. Kurt leaned in closer, his chest pressing against Talia's shoulder as his hand grasped the back of her chair.

"Pause it right there." Kurt pointed to the screen, and then turned to Talia. "Does this man look like he has a mustache?"

She leaned into the monitor closer. The man was just too blurred for her to tell, but it did appear as if hair covered that area between his nose and upper lip.

"In fact," Kurt said softer, "it almost looks like he has a trimmed beard."

As she tried to study the recording, it hit her what Kurt was trying to do. She fisted her hands on her lap and under her breath, counted to ten. When he turned his head to look at her, she glared. "What are you implying?" she muttered between clenched teeth.

"I'm implying that our killer just might have facial hair."

Slowly, she shook her head. "What little we can see of his face is blurred. We can't be sure if it's facial hair or if he just has a mustache and a dirty chin."

Kurt arched an eyebrow. "Seriously? A dirty chin?"

She threw him a glare. "We cannot make an accurate observation, and you know it."

"You're still trying to protect him," he whispered in an accusing tone.

"And you're trying to blame an innocent man." She motioned her head to the monitor. "He probably doesn't even own a black leather jacket. That's not his style."

Kurt's cheeks reddened, and his nostrils flared. "You know his style now?"

"I've had enough." She pushed away from Kurt and stood. Looking at the supervisor, she said, "We'll need this recording to take back with us."

Nodding, the supervisor hurried and pulled out the recording, and then wrote a name and phone number on it. With shaky hands, he gave it to her.

"Thanks for your cooperation." With the recording in hand, she hurried out of the restaurant, not caring if Kurt followed or not.

FOURTEEN

By the time Talia made it to the car, Kurt had caught up. He grabbed her arm, stopping her, and then swung her around to face him. They weren't anywhere near a street lamp, so it was harder to read his expression, especially his eyes.

"Talia," he said, taking deep breaths, "you need to stop this fascination with the perp. Austin Reeder isn't as innocent as you'd like to believe."

She tried to push him away, but he wouldn't let go. Instead, he pulled her closer. "Kurt, I don't want to talk about this right now."

"Talia, sweetheart," he whispered as he caressed her cheek tenderly, "you know I'm right. You know you're not supposed to be feeling this way toward a suspect. If Feakes found out—"

"Don't you dare tell him," she clipped. "And, really… it's not that I'm having feelings for Austin," she lied, "it's just that I feel he's innocent."

"You are having feelings for him. Why else do you think I'd get jealous?" Kurt's voice was softer. "I don't blame you. He's a good-looking man, he's a charmer, and he's rich. What's not to like about him except that he might be a killer."

Tears stung her eyes, but she refused to shed them. Why was Kurt doing this to her? When she was with Austin, her gut – or heart – told her that he wasn't a killer. But when she was with Kurt, the man she'd known longer and trusted with every fiber in her soul, why did doubt sneak in and make her question what her heart believed?

"You just don't understand," she whispered, afraid if she spoke louder, her voice would crack with emotion.

"I understand all too well, sweetheart. I understand my partner – the woman I've come to love – is being brainwashed by a con artist. And I understand it's my duty to protect her all I can by doing whatever is necessary to see the truth."

She fought back the tears, but one slipped through the dam, regardless of how hard she tried not to cry. Her lips trembled, and she didn't dare speak for fear of totally breaking down in front of him.

With the pad of his thumb, he wiped the tear sliding down her cheek. "Let's get in the car."

She nodded. He opened the door for her and helped her inside, then walked around and climbed in the driver's side. He didn't start the car. Instead, he gathered her back into his arms and laid her head against his chest. The position was more awkward now than when they were standing outside, but that was because of the uncomfortable bucket seats and the console between them.

Did he really love her as he'd said? Or did he say that as a way to try to convince her to turn off her feelings for Austin? She really didn't know him that well, and yet, the times they were together, she felt as though they belonged with one another. She was happy with Austin. She was at peace for some reason.

Silence stretched between them for the first few minutes, and all she could hear was the uneven beat of her heart – and his – and his ragged breaths. Her breathing didn't seem to be as irregular. He kissed the top of her head, and she smiled. Her heart softened toward him, once again.

"Sweetheart? Are you going to say anything about what I just told you?"

Inwardly, Talia cringed. It was probably too soon to talk about the L word with Kurt. She loved him, yes, but did she love him like that? At one time she'd wanted to, but he was her partner. He was still her partner.

He cupped her chin and lifted her head until she met his eyes. Shadows were everywhere inside the car, but from the lights on the street, she could see the outline of his face. He was gorgeous. She'd always thought so. She probably always would.

"You know," he said in a deep voice, "I don't have beer breath this time."

She chuckled, even though she didn't want to. She couldn't help it. He had always known how to make her smile or laugh when she was down, just as she knew how to lift his spirits, too.

"No, you don't have beer breath. You have peppermint breath."

"Isn't that better than beer?"

"Tons better."

"So..." He shrugged. "Should we try it again?"

Talia didn't need to ask what he meant. The direction of his gaze was on her mouth. Her heartbeat increased. She couldn't count how many times she had wanted to kiss him, but she knew it would always be in her dreams. And yet, if she kissed Kurt now, would she be betraying Austin? She really did like him, too.

Oh, decisions, decisions...

When he leaned closer, she didn't stop him. She closed her eyes as his lips caressed hers. At first, he hesitated, but when she remained still, he continued. Relaxing into his arms, she kissed him back with the same tenderness he showed to her.

The kiss was nice, and exciting, keeping her heart speeding faster by the second. This was something she'd wanted to do ever since she'd first seen him. And yet, here they were, making out in a parked car, but the man on her mind was Austin. Why couldn't she see Kurt's face in her thoughts?

Slowly, the confusion in her head grew, making her head throb. She needed to end this with Kurt. At least until she could straighten out her thoughts.

She broke the kiss and pulled back. He continued to stare into her eyes as he stroked her face.

"Are you all right?" he asked.

"Yes. I... I just need more time to think about everything."

He nodded and positioned himself behind the steering wheel. He started the car and drove it out of the parking lot. For the first few minutes they were silent, but then he cleared his throat.

"I'm not going to Isabelle's Escort Service now. It's probably too late, anyway. We'll go tomorrow."

"All right."

"Nine o'clock in the morning?"

She nodded. "I'll meet you at the station."

As silence came between them once again, she watched the road and tried to get her thoughts in order. Because her feelings were conflicting with her thoughts, she wanted to scream in frustration. Why did she get this way around Kurt? And why now did he choose this time in her life to confess his love? If only he'd done that before she'd met Austin.

Now what was she going to do? For being a woman who was always in control, she felt as if she was on a spinning ride at the amusement park that had kicked into overdrive. There was only one thing she could do – go and see Austin tonight and finish telling him what she'd started at the waterfront.

She only let Kurt kiss her briefly when he'd returned her to her car. From there she drove to Austin's hotel and hurried up to the penthouse suite. Knocking on the door, she prayed he'd be home, and he'd be alone.

Austin answered the door wearing the same clothes he had on when they'd met at the waterfront. His eyes widened, and he took her arm to pull her inside.

"What are you doing here?" he questioned. "Not that I'm disappointed, though. I'm just surprised."

"I just had to see you tonight. I desperately need to finish our talk that we had earlier."

"I would like that very much. I also have something to share with you." He motioned his hand to the sofa. "But you go first. By the determined look on your face, I assume it's more important than what I have to say."

She nodded and followed him to the sofa. They sat close by each other, which was good. She had always been a touchy-feely person, and she needed that contact with him, if only to help get rid of the confusion still lurking in the dark recesses of her mind.

Once she was comfortable, she took a deep breath of courage. "Austin, I've been hiding something from you since we met, and I can't go another minute without confessing the truth."

Worried lines appeared on his forehead and around his eyes.

She quickly continued. "You're such an awesome person, and I feel you need to know what's really going on with me. I don't want to lie to you any longer, but when you hear my explanation, I hope you'll soon forgive me."

"What's this all about, Talia?"

She swallowed hard and then licked her dry lips. "Before I entered your suite that first day we met, I was waiting for backup so my partner could come in with me. You see, I was given the assignment to interview you, but I was in the middle of my father's engagement party, so I was rather dressed up for the occasion." She swept a hand over her clothes. "This is what I usually wear when I'm fighting criminals. And this," she reached into her purse and pulled out her badge and G42, "is usually what I wear in plain sight while I'm at work."

Pausing, she studied his expression. Just as when she had chased after the purse-snatcher, Austin's face was slowly losing color.

"My partner and I," she quickly resumed, "were supposed to ask you questions in regards to the Kalama Kane case. But when my partner didn't show up, and I heard the thumping noise in your suite, I had no other choice but to go inside to see what was happening. I announced myself, but you didn't respond. Of course, that was when you came out of the bathroom and caught me."

He nodded in hesitation. "Why did you lead me to think you were someone else?"

"When I first saw you, I literally lost my breath." She chuckled lightly. "You'd startled me, but it was more than that. I've never seen a more handsome man in my life, and well, I was at a loss for words, as you could tell. I was extremely embarrassed because of the dress I was wearing, and I realized you wouldn't have believed I was a police detective if I had my gun pulled on you, wearing the red dress. That's another reason why I decided to be someone else. At the time, though, I wasn't sure who you thought I was."

He wore a blank expression as he shook his head. "I'm sure you were quite surprised when I said the things I had."

"You have no idea." She chuckled. "And when I left and met up with my partner later, he was the one who thought I should go undercover to finish collecting information from you. That's why I came to your place yesterday."

His jaw hardened, and the light in his green eyes disappeared. "You were wired when you were with me last night?"

"Yes, in a way. Our conversation was being recorded… well, up until we started arm wrestling. That's when I decided to take out my earpiece."

His gaze narrowed on her. "Why did you want to take it out?"

"Because I didn't want Kurt in my ear any longer."

"Who is Kurt?"

"Oh, he's my partner. Kurt Hamill."

Austin's eyes widened as anger lines appeared around his mouth. She quickly continued, "Anyway, by the time I had taken my earpiece out, I'd decided you hadn't murdered Kalama Kane."

Austin's eyebrows lifted. "Really? You thought that?"

"There's no way a man with your heart and giving nature could be a killer. Besides, I was enjoying my evening with you, and I didn't want my partner to suspect what I was feeling."

"What were you feeling?"

She placed the badge and the Glock inside her purse and zipped it up. "I was starting to really like you." Hesitantly, she looked up and met his wide eyes. "You probably know that it's against the rules for detectives to go out on a date with a suspect."

Austin's face relaxed, and a hint of a smile touched his mouth. "But you don't think I'm a suspect, right?"

"Not anymore."

"Did you collect all the information you needed from me to make that decision?"

Sighing, she rested her hands on her lap. "Not, not exactly. I have one last question to ask."

"What is it?"

"Where were you last Sunday morning between nine-thirty and ten-thirty?" She really didn't have to ask, because she knew he was innocent. But she waited for him to answer, anyway. She wasn't worried.

Finally, recognition shone on his face and he smiled. "I was having a brunch with some of my board members. We were at the hotel in the restaurant. I'm sure your task force will be able to get surveillance footage from the security cameras."

She shrugged one shoulder. "I'm sure they could if they want. I don't need it. I knew you must be preparing for the big forty-eight-hour meeting that you had which made you so exhausted."

He nodded. "You're right. That was it."

So far, this conversation was going the way she'd wanted. He'd acted upset at first, and she didn't blame him, but now he was relaxing more, which made her heart lighten. Leaning toward him, she laid her hand on his chest. "Are you upset at me? I would understand if you were. But it's my job, and well, I'm just glad I got to know you so that I could take you off my suspects' list."

"I'll admit that your confession shocked me, but I suppose if I was in your shoes, I would have done the same." He laughed lightly. "That explains why you were able to take down the purse-snatcher so quickly."

She flipped her hand. "All in a day's work."

He took hold of her hand and placed it back on his chest. "I like it better right here."

Talia's heart danced with excitement. "Me, too."

"Can you tell me why the police think I'm a suspect?"

She nodded. "Kalama had a list of names of men written down in the pocket of her bathrobe. She was killed as soon as she left the bathroom that morning."

He arched an eyebrow. "My name was on that list?"

"Yes."

"But... why?"

"I don't know. I was hoping you could answer that for me. We had figured she was some wealthy man's mistress because she had many expensive items in her house, not to mention a large bank account. All the men on the list were wealthy or powerful."

"I wish I could tell you, unless it's because I gave her money. I don't know. Maybe the other names on the list were men she had contacted for money after I had turned her down."

"That does make sense. I'll have to drop that suggestion to the other detectives." She paused, looking deep into his eyes. The low lighting in the room made his eyes darker than they were normally, and all she wanted to do was stare into his dreamy green eyes. It made her happy that he hadn't kicked her out of his suite, yet.

His gaze moved over her face, and then to her hair. He reached out and caressed the length of the ponytail.

"So, this is really how you look every day at work?" he asked.

"Yes, pretty much."

"How often do you dress up like you had when we first met?"

"Not often." She shook her head. "I've always been more of a tomboy because I grew up with three brothers."

His focus moved down the length of her body this time. "You do look very good in those jeans."

She laughed. "So do you."

"I usually dress up a little more when I go to work."

"Of course, you do. It's not like you have a black leather jacket in your closet. You are the CEO of your own company. I'm just a lowly police detective."

"A police detective," he said, stroking her hair again, "who doesn't take any crap from purse snatchers."

"Exactly."

He was quiet for a few more seconds as he looked her over, and then he tilted his head and met her gaze.

"I suppose I could get used to seeing you wearing this every day."

"You could?" Her hopes grew as she scooted closer to him. "You seem like the kind of man who loves to be seen with the flashy women. I'm not like that. This is as flashy as I like to get."

"Talia," his voice deepened as he brushed his lips across her cheek, "are you trying to convince me we shouldn't go out?"

His warm breath on her neck sent shivers over her body, but instead of feeling cold, she was getting hotter by the second. "I... I just want you to know what you're getting into if you decide to date me."

"I'll admit, it'll be different. I've never gone out with a cop before." His lips moved to her ear.

She closed her eyes as her heartbeat turned ragged. "I've never dated a CEO before."

"I'll give it a try," he kissed her earlobe, "if you can give it a try."

"Hmm, I might be able to do it. I think you'll need to be a little more convincing, though."

His body shook with what she supposed was a silent laugh, and the breath against her neck became hotter. His strong arms circled her body and pulled her up against his muscular frame. Oh... This was so nice!

As his lips moved over her throat, she melted that much more. She couldn't take this torture anymore. If he didn't kiss her soon, she'd scream.

Finally, he lifted his head, but she took that opportunity to find his mouth with hers. The moment their mouths came together, electricity shot through her. If being tasered felt this good, she'd volunteer to be the precinct's dummy next time, but only if Austin could assist her.

She rested her hands against his chest. His heart was knocking as crazily as hers was. Happiness flowed through her knowing he was enjoying this just as much. Strange, but she hadn't felt this kind of energy when she had kissed Kurt not too long ago.

As their kiss turned more passionate, she couldn't keep her fingers still, and she loved the feel of his hair. The urge to run her hands all over him became powerful, but it couldn't happen. This was only their second date.

Breathless, she broke the kiss and leaned her forehead against his chest. "I think... we need to stop."

His chest rattled with a low chuckle. "I agree. We are going too fast. After all, I've only known you as a cop for a few minutes."

"Very true." She tried to breathe slower as her mind returned. "So, Austin. You were going to tell me something, too?"

Confusion crossed his face, but then within seconds, he shook his head. "All I wanted to talk about was us."

"Us?"

"Yes, and where you think we are going."

"Going? Do you mean tonight?" she asked.

He laughed. "No, I'm referring to our relationship – where is it going?"

"Oh." She laid her head on the sofa's cushion. As unbelievable as it sounded, she wanted a relationship with this wonderful man, even if a few days ago she tried to convince herself she didn't have time for a man in her life.

"Let me get through this murder case first, and then I'll be able to think clearly about our relationship."

"All right."

She stood and he held her hand as he walked her to the door.

"You know," he said, "for our next date, I'd really like to see where you live."

Laughing, she threw her arms around his neck and pressed her chest against his. "That's the best idea yet. What are you doing tomorrow night?"

He wagged his eyebrows. "I'll be with you."

FIFTEEN

Kurt awoke in a good mood. He finally felt that Talia was warming up to him. Austin was a difficult competitor, and if this was a race, the rich guy would always win. But as long as Kurt kept reminding her that Austin was still a suspect, maybe, just maybe, she wouldn't fall in love with the man, but with Kurt instead.

He must make sure she never fell in love with Austin. Men like that deserved to spend the rest of their life in prison. Men like Austin believed themselves to be above the law. Men like Austin were one of the reasons Kurt became a policeman in the first place.

Kurt's father wasn't a great example of being an upright citizen in the community, either. When he divorced Kurt's mother, his father married a wealthy woman, just for her money. That still didn't make him want to pay child support. The few times Kurt had visited his father, it seemed like the new wife and her son walked around as if they owned the town. Kurt always kept an eye on his stepbrother. That kid was sneaky, especially in school. Kurt wondered if he was paying the teachers just to pass him to the next grade.

His stepbrother always seemed to get girls, which didn't surprise Kurt at all since all those girls saw were dollar signs. His stepbrother enjoyed flaunting his wealth – and women – in front of Kurt. In all those years, he kept reminding himself he was the better person. Once he turned eighteen, he was able to decide for himself whether or not he wanted to be part of his dad's life. Kurt decided against it. He didn't need that kind of influence.

Only one good thing came out of knowing his father's new family. It had instilled the determination inside Kurt to become a policeman and capture crafty criminals who thought they were above the law and throw them in the slammer.

Kurt waited impatiently for Talia to arrive. Every two minutes, he kept checking the clock. She was never late, but if she didn't walk in the door any second now, she would be breaking her own record.

His conscience still nagged at him, reminding him that Talia was his partner. He shouldn't become romantically involved with her. There were too many horror stories of things like that happening on the force. Being attracted to one's partner made police officers do sloppy work. They couldn't think clearly, which of course, a good police detective needed in this line of work.

"Are you ready?"

The sweet voice jerked him from staring at his computer as he looked up at Talia. She dressed like she did every day, wearing dark blue jeans that hugged her hips, and a nice blouse, and her sensible walking shoes. And always, she pulled her hair back into a ponytail. But there was something different about her countenance. There was a certain twinkle in her brown eyes, and a lift to her heart-shaped lips.

Silently, he cheered. He'd bet anything that she looked this way because of the kiss they'd shared last night. He definitely had a bounce in his step and happiness in his heart because of their kiss.

"Yes, I'm ready." He pushed away from the desk and stood. "Are you driving or do you want me to drive?"

"I'll drive." She jiggled her keys.

He smiled. He liked when she drove, mainly because it gave him more time to admire her profile. Plain and simple, he loved just watching her.

"Have you heard anything about the other suspects?" she asked, climbing into the car.

As soon as he sat and tightened his seatbelt around him, he turned toward her. "Yes. We know that Robert Phipps and Kevin Shupe are pricey lawyers. Both Reeder and Chad Johnson are wealthy. Tim Beaton is a congressman, and Lenny Lytle is the mayor's son. Each man except one has an alibi."

"Have the alibi's been checked out?" Talia asked without looking at him as she merged into traffic.

"Yes, and they all seem legit. But, Talia... Reeder is the only one who hasn't given us his alibi."

Her jaw hardened, and her fingers tightened around the steering wheel. "I got it last night."

Kurt held his breath as his heart began to slowly crumble. "You... went without me?"

"Kurt," her shoulders sagged, but she continued to keep her eyes on the road, "I had a gut feeling that Austin wasn't guilty, so last night after I left you, I went to see him. I..." Her throat lurched. "I told him the truth about my identity."

"You what?" Anger rose inside him and he fisted his hands. Several times during their year-long partnership, he'd wanted to shake some sense into the headstrong woman. Now was certainly one of those moments.

"I would have told him eventually. You know how I feel about lying."

He gritted his teeth. "Did he give you his alibi before or after you told him the truth?"

"After."

Inwardly, he growled. "Talia, how do you know he wasn't lying?"

"Kurt," her fingers moved on the steering wheel as if she was trying to choke something, "I know you have something against Austin, but I feel deep in my gut that he was telling the truth."

"What was his alibi?" he snapped.

"Remember when I told you that he'd been in a merger that had lasted forty-eight hours, and that's the reason he was in his penthouse suite when I walked in on him?"

"Yes."

"Well, before the merger started, he was having breakfast with some of his board members. That's where he was around the time Kalama Kane was killed."

"Make sure you get a list of names of these board members so we can check Reeder's alibi."

"Seriously, Kurt?" She shook her head. "I honestly can't believe you don't trust my word or my feelings."

"And I can't believe," he countered back, "that you'd go behind my back to get his alibi. We are supposed to be a team and do this together."

She sat in silence as she drove. He hoped she was thinking about his words. He just couldn't let this one go. Proving Austin's guilt was necessary now. How else could he prove to Talia how wrong she'd been about the guy?

"What worries me," he continued, "is you're letting Reeder's handsome face, buff body, and especially, his bank account, sway your thoughts. He's just a normal man, you know. He's not some Greek God women like to put on a pedestal. He makes mistakes just like the rest of us."

Finally, she briefly looked away from the road to toss him a scowl. "Kurt, what has that man ever done to you? Why are you acting this way?"

"I'm trying to make you see that just because he has a pretty smile doesn't make him higher-than-thou perfect. He may just be our killer. You just never know."

Grumbling, she turned into a parking lot, eyeing the strip of businesses. One of the signs read: Isabella's Escort Service.

"We're here," she clipped.

They walked into the building without speaking a word to each other. Perhaps the only way to convince Talia that she was allowing her attraction to run her thoughts instead of her head was to hold her and kiss her as he'd done last night.

The blonde bombshell with a shapely figure and low-cut blouse that showed an ample view of her bosom, sitting at the receptionist's desk, smiled up at them. Kurt was surprised that her bright red lipstick wasn't smudged on her white teeth.

"Good morning," she said almost seductively. "Welcome to Isabella's Escort Service. How may I help you?"

Both Kurt and Talia flashed their badges. Kurt began, "We're HPD Detectives, and we'd like to talk to the owner of this establishment."

The woman's eyes grew wide. "Umm... well, Mr. Martin is not here at the moment. Can I schedule you an appointment to meet with him?"

"No," Talia quickly answered. "You can tell us when he'll be in next so we can come back."

"Umm... let me check his calendar." Her hand shook as she scrolled through the computer screen. "It looks like he'll be back around four-thirty."

Kurt exchanged glances with Talia and slowly shook his head. He reached into his jacket and pulled out the photo of Kalama Kane. He showed it to the receptionist. "What do you know about this woman?"

"I... umm, I don't know anything."

Talia rolled her eyes. "How long have you worked for this office?"

"About five years."

"Then you know her." Talia pointed to the picture. "Because she worked for this escort service up until about two years ago. And by my calculations, that would mean she would have worked here while you were here."

Color disappeared from the woman's face. Kurt guessed this woman to be in her early twenties. He pushed the picture closer to the woman. Her gaze narrowed as if she were studying the picture. It was obvious by the woman's expression, that she knew Kalama.

"Oh, yes." The woman gave a forced laugh. "That's Kalama Kane. I remember her now."

Talia smiled and slowly nodded. "I'm relieved to know your memory returned so quickly."

The woman's gaze moved to Kurt. She leaned forward on the desk, giving him a peek show of her plunging neckline. She batted her fake eyelashes and gave him another toothy smile. "What do you want to know about Kalama? She hasn't been around this place in like forever."

"Define for me your phrase, *in like forever.*" He arched an eyebrow. "How long exactly is that?"

She laughed in a flirty way and flipped a lock of her blonde hair over her shoulder. "It means, handsome, that once she quit, she hasn't been back since."

He'd known so many women like this one. They believed all they had to do was show a man a little skin, pout, and bat their eyelashes, and they'd get anything. That's definitely not how he liked to work.

"When she worked here," he continued, "did she have a lot of clients?"

She gave that faulty laugh again. "Oh, detective, you must not know the way things work in this office. The girls don't own their clients. Men or women come in here seeking companionship, and we assign them to the type of woman or man that fits them best."

"Let me rephrase that," Kurt said, "I need a list of clients that were assigned to Kalama a lot."

She giggled. "I'm sorry, detective, but I can't give you that."

Talia stepped closer to the woman and glared. "You will once we get a warrant."

The receptionist scowled and pulled back. "Then I'll wait until you can show me one."

Kurt motioned his head toward the door, silently communicating with Talia. She turned and walked away from the desk. He glanced back at the receptionist. "Tell Mr. Martin we'll be back at four-thirty with a warrant to get the records we need."

When he turned back to Talia, she stood next to the door, studying some photos on the wall. Most of the pictures were that of the outdoors, but in two of them was the same man. She waited until he stopped by her side before she led them outside and toward the door.

"I've seen that man in the photo before," Talia said once they were far enough away from the building. "I also believe I've seen that woman, too."

"The ditzy receptionist?" he asked.

"Yes."

"Where?"

"I'm not sure just yet. I'll think about it."

She hurried to the car and climbed inside. Once he was in, she looked at him. "I think we're going to need that search warrant."

"Me, too. Let's just hope we can convince Judge Peterson. She's hardheaded."

Talia chuckled. "Oh, Kurt. She has always liked you. I bet all you have to do is give the judge your knee-buckling grin and she'll issue that warrant."

Grinning, he shook his head. "It won't work this time, because I'm not wearing the shirt with the low neckline." He grinned.

Talia snorted a laugh and started the car. "I just worry that it might be too late. What if Miss Ditz inside deletes all of Kalama's clients?"

"Then we'll arrest her for tampering with evidence."

"Oh, let's hope that happens," Talia said with a laugh. "I really want to bust that woman for something."

"If I had my way, I'd bust her for indecent exposure."

She laughed and placed her hand on the gear shift, but Kurt reached up to stop her. When her eyes met his, he leaned in closer.

"I like this."

"Like what?" she asked in a small voice.

"I like being silly with you. I like that I can make you smile, and I love it when you can make me laugh."

Her smile relaxed. "I've always enjoyed these moments, too."

"I want more of them."

Sighing, she sank back in the seat, resting her fingers on the bottom of the steering wheel. She stared at her fingers instead of looking at him.

"Kurt, I don't want to fight with you anymore. I don't want to argue about who is guilty and who is innocent. I want us both to look at the evidence and use that as our guide to which perp needs to be brought in."

He touched her chin, moving her face toward his. When her eyes locked with his, he nodded. "I can do it if you can."

"I can do it."

"Good. And now that we have that out of the way, there's one more thing I want to discuss."

"What's that?"

"This." He closed the space between them and placed his lips on hers. She sucked in a quick breath, but within moments, she relaxed. As she moved her lips back and forth with his, he slipped an arm around her waist. He knew this wasn't the place to make-out, even though it would be enjoyable. But he just needed a kiss. This one – as short as it was – would suffice for now.

He pulled away, adjusted his seat, and pulled on his seatbelt. "Where to next?"

"Back to the station. We have some evidence to go over, again, and more people to interview today."

He nodded. "Excellent plan."

Deep in his heart, he knew things would work out with him and Talia. All they needed was to communicate better.

SIXTEEN

Voices of Austin's board members filled the room in heavy discussion about the upcoming takeover, but Austin couldn't concentrate. He hadn't stopped thinking about Talia, especially now that she told him about being a police detective. Why hadn't he seen that coming? Apparently, she was a really good actress... or he was extremely naïve.

Part of him wanted to trust her with all of his heart, but there was always that niggle of doubt in the back of his mind. Life's experiences taught him that the task force treated wealthy people differently. For some reason, they had it in their minds that wealthy people tend to ignore the law. Austin worried Talia would have this attitude, as well.

Why he had fallen so fast and hard for this amazing woman, he didn't know. It would certainly break his heart if he couldn't trust her.

Yesterday, he'd wanted to confess something to her about his relationship with Kalama Kane, but once Talia had admitted her true identity, he didn't dare say anything. Not now. Not until he knew without a doubt, that he could trust her.

And then there was the problem with Kurt Hamill. Austin would never trust that particular cop. Austin had learned a long time ago who was trustworthy and who would stab him in the back with a sharp blade. Kurt Hamill was the type of man who would run Austin over in a car, and then back up and drive over him again, just for pure satisfaction.

Finally, at long last, the board meeting ended. Austin stuffed his files inside his leather briefcase and moved away from the table. He didn't want to chat with the others, so he made his apologies and quickened his step, hurrying out of the building. Just before reaching his charcoal colored, classic 911 SC Porsche, his cell rang. He checked the caller ID. What was Ariki calling him for?

"Hello," Austin answered.

"Hey. Can you talk?"

"Briefly. What's up?"

"I have another girl I want to set you up with."

Austin grinned. "Thanks for thinking about me, but I'm good."

"What do you mean *you're good*? Did you and that Talia woman hook up?"

"Yes."

"And… you're not tired of her yet?"

Austin wanted to laugh out loud, but his friend was probably used to calling him every week to set him up with a new woman.

"No, Ariki. Talia Russell is a fascinating woman. I think I'll keep her around just a little longer."

Silence hung on the other end of the phone for a few seconds. Then Ariki gasped. "Russell? Did you say her last name was Russell?"

"Yes, why?"

Ariki muttered a cuss. "Reeder, I can't believe it. Just a few moments ago, a woman by that name came along with a male detective, and dropped by my place to ask questions about you and Kalama Kane."

"What?" Stunned, Austin stood frozen by his car with the door open. "Why would they talk to you?"

Ariki huffed. "Because I guess you had mentioned my name as someone who sets you up with women. They think I'm a pimp or something."

Austin wanted to laugh, but he refrained. He was too upset to find humor in Ariki's new title. It infuriated Austin to think Talia and her idiot partner had the nerve to question Ariki. What possible evidence would Ariki have had?

"I'll handle this," Austin snapped and climbed into his car. "Those detectives have stepped way over the line this time."

"So Reeder? What's going on? Do they really suspect you in that murder case just because you knew Kalama?"

"Ariki, I'll talk to you later. Right now, I need to find someone and get the answers myself." Austin clicked off the phone without waiting for his friend's reply.

Anger fueled his actions, and he stomped on the gas pedal, going faster than he should. Zipping in and out of traffic, he focused on one thing. Finding Talia.

* * * *

Talia walked into her apartment and closed the door. Leaning against the thick piece of wood, she blew out a sigh of despair. She had thrown herself into her job today, mainly to keep her mind off Austin and Kurt and the confusing feelings she'd experienced with them lately.

Kurt's words this morning had got her thinking, which at this point in a relationship could be very dangerous. Had she fallen in love with Austin because he was rich? Was it because of his incredible good looks and charm? She had never fallen for a man so quickly, so why had she done it this time?

Rubbing her throbbing head, she walked into her living room and plopped down onto the couch. She'd been too busy to think of her feelings for these two men, but now she was exhausted from everything she'd accomplished. The detectives in the precinct had interviewed more people, and from these interviews, they'd gotten more leads. But they still weren't any closer to finding Kalama Kane's killer.

Kurt, Tyrone and Gibbs leaned more toward Austin and Chad Johnson, mainly because they were rich. She happened to think the congressman's son, Tim Beaton, had a questionable alibi.

Nothing made sense. While she was interviewing leads, Kurt tried to find out everyone in Honolulu that might have a collection of medieval weapons. The medical examiner had the broken piece, so all they needed to do was to find the rest of the weapon in hopes of catching the murderer.

Around four-thirty, they had returned to Isabella's Escort Service only to find it had been closed for the day. Figures. Both she and Kurt knew that escort business was hiding something. Apparently, they were trying to conceal the owner, Mr. Martin. What other things haven't they disclosed?

A knock came upon the door. Hesitantly, she trudged across the room to see who had come. Instead of looking through the peephole this time, she just opened the door. Austin stood in front of her, holding a bouquet of red roses. Her heart softened to see him after such a long and grueling day, but her heart leapt with happiness that he was thoughtful and brought her flowers, too.

"Austin! What a surprise. Please, come in."

He walked in and she closed the door. Shaking her head in confusion, she took the flowers he handed to her.

"How did you know where I lived? Or did I give you my address and just forgot?"

"I was leaving the flower shop when I saw you drive past. I quickly jumped into my car and followed you." He stepped closer to her and stroked her cheek. "I hope you don't mind if I start our date a little earlier than planned."

"Not at all. Thank you so much for the flowers. I'll put them in a vase." She moved into the kitchen to look through her cupboards. She had a vase once, but she couldn't remember where she placed it.

"So, this is where you live?" he asked as he walked toward her living room.

"Yes. It's nothing fancy." *Oh, there's a vase.* She carefully placed the roses inside.

He tsked and shook his head before looking over his shoulder and grinning wide. "And to think, you turned down a penthouse suite for this."

She laughed. "Exactly. Now you can see why, right?"

He moved back to her at the counter by the sink as she filled the vase with water.

"Yes, I can see why you wouldn't be able to give up a place like this. Creaky floors, chipped walls and ceilings. Warped cupboards in the kitchen. And if I'm not mistaken," he glanced at the sink's faucet, "a dripping problem to go along with the other extra bonuses that came with the apartment."

She playfully slugged him in the arm. "Right, and it's all mine for only eight-hundred dollars a month."

"You certainly live in a fairy-tale, don't you?" He winked.

"But of course. That's the only way to make it through the day – to pretend I'm in a fairy-tale." Closing her eyes, she opened her arms wide and sighed.

"Am I your Prince Charming?" he asked, closing the space between them as he circled his arms around her.

She released another sigh, heavier and more meaningful this time, cuddling against his chest. "Definitely, you're my Prince Charming."

He stroked the length of her ponytailed hair. "Then you shall be my Princess Charming."

Giggling, she peered up into his seducing gaze. "Princess Charming? Who in the world is that?"

"It's whoever you want to be, sweet lady."

"For tonight, I just want to be myself with you."

He kissed her forehead. "Do you want me to take you out to eat?"

"Actually," she caressed his muscular chest, "if you don't mind, I want to stay right here with you. We can have dinner here. I'll order pizza or Chinese delivery. Which one do you want?"

He gave her a crooked grin. "Would you think I'm a snob if I confess I haven't had pizza or Chinese delivered to me for many years?"

"No, I wouldn't think that way about you." She pulled out of his embrace, "However, I think you're going to love either one of them. The nearby restaurants in this area have the best food."

"Which one are you hungry for?" he asked.

"It doesn't matter to me." She shrugged. "Chinese?"

"Get it ordered."

She pulled out her cell and dialed the number she had on speed dial, and ordered two of the specials of the day. Because she liked anything that came from their restaurant, she knew she'd eat it. And of course, being a special meant it was two dollars off the regular price.

When she was finished and placed the phone back in her pocket, she noticed Austin had made himself comfortable on her couch. He sure looked handsome tonight. Then again, he always looked handsome. But he wasn't quite as dressy as she'd seen him before. He wore dark blue Levis that appeared brand new, and his normal dressy baby blue shirt and tie. But his tie was loosened and the top two buttons on his shirt were undone.

He motioned for her to sit beside him, so she did. Once on the couch, he slid his arm around her shoulders, pulling her closer.

"Tell me, what do you usually accomplish most evenings when you're home alone?"

"Accomplish?" She laughed. "Not much. Some days I do the laundry, but the other times I do nothing but watch TV. I might open my laptop and check my emails or other social media sites, but I'm pretty much a dull person who sits around and does nothing."

He frowned. "I can't remember the last time I sat around doing nothing."

"What is your evening like when you get home from work?"

"Well," he said, stretching his legs out as he scooted down onto the couch, bringing her with him, "I look over papers from the several meetings I'd attended that day. I answer my phone messages, and if I have time after that, I check my emails and answer those."

She cuddled against him, lying on her side and placing her leg over his. This felt so nice. Too nice, in fact. She could get used to this if she wasn't careful. Then again, maybe that's what she really wanted to do. "When do you eat?"

"When I get hungry." He chuckled. "But I usually just order room service."

"You poor man." She stroked his trimmed beard. "You really need to get out more."

Laughing, he gathered her closer, pulling her body onto his chest a little more. "That's why I'm with you. I want you to show me the world."

Her cheeks warmed from his compliment, and that wasn't the only thing warming up. The position they were in was too darn cozy, and very personal. Yet, she didn't want to move. Ever. She wondered why he wasn't trying to kiss her yet. The other times she'd been with him, he was always the one starting the kiss. She really couldn't let this intimate moment between them go to waste, could she?

"I can definitely show you my world." Sighing, she leaned up and placed her lips on his. At first, it was almost as if he was hesitant to kiss her, but she didn't pull away. After the confusing day she'd had, she wanted him to take her mind off everything so she could focus only on him.

Finally, he relaxed and kissed her passionately, exciting her more as the seconds passed. He held her head while their mouths moved together. This was pure magic.

She couldn't do a lot with her hands since they were trapped between their chests, but she reached his tie and finished loosening it and slipping it off from around his neck. When her fingers moved to the third button on his shirt, she felt his hands move on her head, back to her ponytail. After a few tugs of her tie, her hair fell down around her shoulders, and around their joined faces, shrouding them from the outside world.

His hands moved again, threading through her long hair. This seemed to kick him into a higher gear because his kisses became faster, more urgent. The excitement building inside of her was almost to inferno status. Did he know how much she enjoyed kissing him like this – like there was no tomorrow, and nobody else in this world besides Austin and Talia?

But before she could do anymore, he shifted, breaking the kiss. His breath was as ragged as her own. Staring deep into her eyes, he swallowed hard.

He caressed her cheek. "You are so hard to resist."

"Why are you resisting, then?" She couldn't believe the husky voice that just answered was really hers. And she also couldn't believe the words that had exited her mouth. Was she challenging him to do more? Then again, he was her Prince Charming, wasn't he?

He took a deep breath. As he slowly released the breath, he smiled. "Because I want to talk now. We are still getting to know each other, aren't we?"

"Yes."

"So, let's start now." He breathed deeply and slowly once more. "Tell me everything you did today, everyone you talked to, everywhere you went. I want to know how a police detective works."

"Seriously?" She, too, tried to calm her speeding heartrate, and tried to regulate her breathing, too. "You want to know what I did today?"

"Just you, sweet lady. Only you."

"Do you really think I can remember all of that?"

"I think you can remember that and more." He winked.

She really didn't want to mention names, but she figured calling them by their first name wouldn't hurt. Besides, Austin probably wouldn't know half of these people. As she began to tell him about her day, it surprised her how interested he appeared, like he was hanging on her every word. She loved feeling that important. He definitely made her feel this way quite a bit lately.

His forehead creased a little as his wide smile slowly disappeared. "Did you talk to Ariki?"

She pulled up slightly. "Ariki? Your friend, Ariki?"

"Yes."

She shook her head. "Why would I talk to Ariki?"

Austin shrugged. "Because he also knew Kalama."

"Well, unless Ariki was a name on her list, or unless he was a lead, we wouldn't have asked him any questions."

"But, someone talked to him. He said it was you."

She blinked with wide eyes, sitting up a little more. "If I talked to him, I didn't know who he was. I told you everyone I had spoken with. I haven't even met your friend. Why would you think that?"

"Because he mentioned earlier—"

Talia's cell buzzed. Groaning, she climbed off him, and the couch, to pull it out of her pocket. "Russell here."

Austin blew out a gush of air and sank further in the cushions as he stared up at the ceiling.

"Talia, I think we found something," Kurt said breathlessly.

"What did you find?"

"Gibbs interviewed one of Reeder's board members, and guess who is a collector of medieval weapons?"

She turned away from Austin, stepping closer to the kitchen. "Who?"

"Our very own Austin Reeder. I'm getting a search warrant ready as we speak. We'll be able to search his place tonight."

SEVENTEEN

Kurt paced the front of the hotel, waiting for Talia to arrive. Reeder wasn't here, either, and Kurt had a bad feeling the two were together. If they showed up together, he didn't know what he'd do. It would certainly crush his heart because then he'd know she hadn't cared enough to ponder his suggestion earlier today.

When Feakes and the others arrived, Kurt realized they would be searching Reeder's suite without her.

Feakes marched toward Kurt, pointing toward the front doors of the hotel. "Let's do this." Then the sergeant stopped and glanced around. "Where's Russell?"

"She'll be here."

"I'm not going to wait for her to powder her nose."

Gritting his teeth, Kurt held back the remarks he'd wanted to fling at his supervisor. Why did the man have to always pick on Talia? Kurt wished he knew.

Out of the corner of his eyes, he saw Talia's Jetta squeal into the parking lot. He sighed with relief, and pointed in that direction. "She's here," he told Feakes.

"Good." Feakes nodded. "Let's go."

She practically jumped out of her vehicle, and marched Kurt's way. By the stern expression on her face, he would be arguing with her very soon. At least he had the others to back him up. She could yell at him all night, but the fact was, the detectives finally got a lead they could count on. Without the murder weapon, how could they truly convict the killer? The other men must have noticed, because they quickened their step inside the hotel.

"Kurt Hamill!" she shouted. "What do you think you're doing?"

"I told you on the phone." He turned and tried to follow the other detectives. "Gibbs talked to one of Reeder's board members—"

"Why was Gibbs talking to one of the board members?"

Kurt rolled his eyes. "Because, sweetheart, that's what we do when we check up on suspects' alibis."

"And did this board member confirm that Austin was with them?"

"Yes, but he wasn't sure what time it actually was. He thought it could have been later than ten, which means—"

"I know what that means. Was he the only one Gibbs questioned? I'm assuming the words board members are plural. Gibbs should have asked more than one person."

"Talia, will you stop interrupting me, and listen to what I have to say?" They walked into the elevator and Talia pushed the button for the top floor. "The board member told Gibbs that he's like an art dealer. He finds ancient artifacts and sells them to wealthy people. Reeder just happens to be one of those people. Fred Cheek said he sold a medieval weapon to Reeder only four months ago. The artifact is called Indian Shispar. It's a flanged mace – the exact weapon that killed Kalama Kane."

She glared at him. "I know what the weapon is called."

He held up his hands in surrender. "You don't need to bite my head off."

Grumbling incoherently, she raked her fingers through her long hair and looked down at the floor. His mind went into overdrive. Why wasn't her hair in a ponytail? She really shouldn't have taken it out. With her hair long and flowing like this, it made her that much more desirable.

"I just don't understand you, sometimes," she said, after a few seconds of silence. "Austin has a perfect alibi, and yet you're still determined to search his apartment for the weapon." She met his gaze again. "Have you forgotten I was in there a few times? I didn't see any weapons."

Kurt leaned back against the wall and folded his arms. "Did you get to see all of his rooms? If I remember correctly, you were only in the living room and the kitchen and dining areas."

Huffing, she turned back to look at the electronic board as it counted each floor, giving off a small ding when they reached a floor. He wished she wouldn't be like this. What else could he do to make her see that Austin Reeder wasn't the man she thought he was?

"Were you with Reeder tonight?" Kurt finally asked the question that had been on his mind tonight.

"That's none of your business," she snapped without looking at him.

Kurt knew she had been. She didn't need to say it. The crushing weight in his chest pressed down harder, making it difficult to breathe. He couldn't let this affect him. Not until after they'd searched the perp's penthouse suite.

Just as they reached the top floor, and the elevator doors opened, the second set of elevator doors also dinged and opened. Kurt watched to see who exited the elevator, because he knew the rest of the detectives were already here.

Austin Reeder walked out, his face red with anger. The perp glanced at the other detectives waiting at the front door, and then he moved his attention to Kurt. A scowl crossed the perp's face.

"What do you guys want now?" Reeder growled.

Kurt motioned toward the door. "We have a search warrant. We would like you to open the door and let us in so we can do our job."

Feakes moved forward to present Reeder with the signed warrant from Judge Peterson. Reeder switched his gaze to Talia, and his frown deepened. Kurt didn't want to look at Talia's face, because he knew it would show the pain and frustration she obviously shared with Austin. Kurt couldn't take seeing her look so broken.

Reeder opened his door and motioned his arms for them to enter. The detectives moved inside, each going to a separate corner of the room. Kurt went ahead of Talia. When he received his first glance at the wealthy man's room, he tried not to let his jaw drop in awe. Then again, why would Austin Reeder live any other way? He had luxury when he was younger, so why not now?

When Austin walked past Kurt, he shook his head. "I should have known you were behind this. You always saw the worst in me, and my mother."

The loud gasp from Talia jerked Kurt's head her way. Her eyes were wide and accusing as she moved her gaze between him and Austin.

"You two… know each other?"

Austin arched a judgmental eyebrow. "I'm surprised your partner didn't tell you sooner Talia, but yes, we know each other. His father married my mother when I was ten years old."

Kurt shook his head. "I never wanted to be related to you, and I feel even stronger about it now."

"Kurt, why… why… didn't you tell me," Talia sobbed out the words. Tears formed in her eyes and her bottom lip quaked.

He wasn't going to feel guilty over this no matter how much he loved her. "Talia, I had never approved of him or his mother. They both thought themselves to be above the law." He tossed a glare at Austin. "You were the reason I wanted to become a cop, so I could put wealthy and crooked men like you away behind bars. Your mother should have gone to jail for tax evasion, and you…" Kurt shook his head. "You should have gone to jail for just being a liar. I can't count how many times you lied just to get out of doing things. Your whole life has been one big lie."

Austin shook his head. "I don't know what I ever did to you to make you feel this way. I may have paid a few people in school to do my homework assignments, but that's as far as I got when it comes to cheating. Just because you didn't like me, you had to make up stories to tell my parents. Thankfully, your father never believed you. Hamill, I have never been deceitful. My mother has, yes, but I'm nothing like her."

Kurt snickered. "Yeah, tell it to the judge."

Kurt moved past him to assist his co-workers in finding the weapon. But within seconds, Tyrone's voice was heard from one of the rooms. "I found it!"

Before Kurt could think to move, Talia pushed past him with Reeder close on her heels. Kurt passed a bathroom, a bedroom, and a den, before coming to the last room. This was where Reeder kept his collection. Not only were there several pieces of medieval weapons, but there was an assortment of all kinds of weapons from ancient times. If he wasn't so elated to know they finally found the murder weapon, he'd be in awe of all of the priceless artifacts in this room.

Tyrone held up the flanged mace. Feakes was standing close, examining the sharp tips of the weapon, especially the area where the sharp edge was missing. The sergeant nodded and carefully slid a large, clear bag over the top. This piece would be added to the other evidence involved with this case.

Standing in shock, Austin shook his head. "I didn't do it. I'm not a killer!"

Feakes shot the perp a heated scowl. "Hamill, cuff Mr. Money-bags and bring him down to the station for questioning."

"I want my lawyer present." Austin stood firm.

"Your lawyer will be present." Feakes nodded. "But we need to dust this for fingerprints, and also get your fingerprints."

Kurt waited for the sergeant and the others to walk out of the room. Talia didn't leave. Her face had lost color, and her eyes were filled with tears as she stared at Austin.

The perp shook his head. "You have to believe me, Talia. I didn't kill Kalama. I'm just an artifact collector, not a murderer."

Kurt grasped Reeder's wrists, pulling them behind his back and hooking on the handcuffs. "Let's go, Reeder. We need to ask you some questions about the murder of Kalama Kane."

Hanging his head, Reeder allowed Kurt to lead him out of the room. Finally, Kurt would get to see his stepbrother humiliated and get what he deserved. Kurt couldn't believe the happiness that flowed through him right now. How many years had he waited for this moment? How many times had he seen rich guys pay their way out of crimes? Well, Kurt would personally see to it that Reeder couldn't use his money for this bail out.

EIGHTEEN

You are a professional. You can do this! Talia fought the emotions twisting inside of her as she willed herself not to cry again. Feakes could see she'd become too involved with Austin to handle the questioning. Even the sergeant wouldn't allow Kurt into the interrogation room, either, since they knew each other growing up.

As she paced back and forth in the observation room, she listened closely to every question Gibbs and Tyrone were asking Austin. So far, she'd known these answers. Austin knew Kalama… she tried to get him as one of her clients, but he refused… he was in a board meeting that morning she was killed… blah, blah, blah.

Her heart broke with each question the detectives threw at Austin. Sometimes his lawyer would cut in and tell Austin he didn't have to answer that, but Austin always answered. He kept repeating that he didn't kill Kalama. Deep inside of her, she believed him. But why did he have the murder weapon?

The fingerprint results came back on the weapon, and there were many prints that were smudged, and some were overlapping, but the one good print they found was Austin's. He didn't deny handling the weapon, because, obviously, he purchased it and set it upon the shelf.

"Mr. Reeder, who do you go through to do your banking?"

Talia paused and looked into the window. Austin's forehead creased and his gaze narrowed. Where was Tyrone going with this?

"Aloha Pacific Bank. Why? That's not a secret. Most people bank there."

Tyrone and Gibbs exchanged grins. Talia's heart dropped.

"Mr. Reeder, we found something interesting on Kalama Kane' bank statement. She doesn't go through Aloha Pacific, however, earlier this year, that very bank was depositing one thousand dollars in her account every month for three months." Tyrone cocked his head, staring at Austin. "By chance, was that money coming from you?"

Talia growled and swung around. She looked at Kurt first, and then switched her attention to Feakes. "Seriously? What does that have to do with anything?"

"I'm sure we'll find out." Feakes pointed to the window.

Austin remained silent, even when his lawyer leaned over and whispered something in his ear. Nodding, Austin cleared his throat and straightened his shoulders.

"Yes. I had sent her one-thousand dollars for three months."

Talia's knees weakened and she fell against the wall. Kurt rushed to her side, but she pushed him away. This all had to be a nightmare. Hadn't Austin been honest with her at all during their few short dates? Apparently not, or she would have known all of this.

"Why, Mr. Reeder? Was she blackmailing you?" Gibbs probed. "Did she know one of your deep, dark secrets and was going to expose it to the community?"

Austin's expression grew hard and his nostrils flared. Several seconds passed without him saying anything, until finally, he nodded.

"She knew something about me that not many people know."

Gibbs and Tyrone exchanged knowing glances. Talia wanted to smack their assured smiles off their faces.

"And… what is that?" Gibbs asked.

Austin released a heavy breath and raked his fingers through his hair. "I'm not who I appear to be in the community."

Talia held her breath. What was he talking about?

"And who are you exactly, Mr. Reeder?" Gibbs urged.

"I'm a successful man, and I've worked hard to get where I am. People know me as the CEO who owns hotels and resorts, but what they don't know is that I own islands, too. I have two personal planes, and several cars and limos. I have estates all over the world. I give thousands of dollars to charities. I'm an art collector, but my assets are worth… *billions.*" He arched an eyebrow. "I'm a billionaire, and not many people know it."

Gasps were heard from Kurt and Feakes, and of course, from the detectives in the interrogation room, but all she could do was stare at him through the mirrored window. Tears filled her eyes as her heart continued to break. Why hadn't he told her?

Tyrone shook his head. "I don't quite understand you, Reeder. You're a billionaire, and yet you don't live like one. Why?"

Austin's expression was blank when he stared at Tyrone. "Because I didn't want to be treated differently. I wanted women to love me for myself and not for my bank account."

Another tear slid down Talia's cheek, but she kept her eyes – and ears – on the interrogation room.

"Kalama wanted some of your billions, eh?" Gibbs asked.

"No. That's not what happened. You've got it all wrong." Austin didn't take his stare off Gibbs.

The pounding in Talia's head grew stronger. She was going to be sick, she just knew it.

"It wasn't? So, you're telling me she wasn't your mistress? Tell us, Reeder." Tyrone asked, moving closer. "Besides being a billionaire, what else did she know about you that would make you want to kill her?"

"I did not kill her," Austin said in a loud voice. "How many times do I have to tell you that? I was with a few board members that morning. Why isn't this sinking in that thick skull of yours yet?"

Tyrone leaned on the table, putting his face right in front of Austin. "Then tell us why you were paying her blackmail money."

Austin's gaze shifted toward the window. Talia knew he couldn't see her, but he certainly knew she was watching. He looked back at the other detectives, and then sighed heavily.

"Kalama was my cousin."

Talia released a high-pitched gasp, and then quickly covered her mouth with her hands. *Cousins?* That couldn't be right. He made her believe he had dated Kalama at one time, and that had turned into friendship later on. Why didn't he tell her? What was so important to keep that a secret?

"Her mother and my father were siblings," Austin continued. "Kalama came to me one day a few years ago, explaining how she'd gotten involved with Belle's Escort Service, and she needed help getting out. I gave her some money. I even talked to the owner and paid them to let her go. Then a few months ago, she told me she had gotten into another scrape and needed help. Once again, I dished out money to help her. It lasted for three months, and then I stopped the payment. When she came to see me and ask why, I told her I wasn't going to help her any longer. We argued, and she left. End... of... story!"

Gibbs shook his head. "No, Reeder. There has to be more to the story. Why were you on her list?"

Austin's face turned red. "I don't know. Why don't you ask her?"

"Oh, really funny, Reeder." Tyrone snickered.

"Listen," Austin continued, "one of the things she told me the day we argued was that she was trying to get money from other men, but they weren't helping her."

Gibbs and Tyrone glanced at each other and then moved their attention back to Austin. "What men?"

"She didn't tell me their names. But if she played the oh-pity-me card on them, I'm sure they were giving her money, too. So why aren't they here? Why are you wasting your time with me instead of finding the real killer?"

"Because none of those other men had the murder weapon in their house," Tyrone said loudly.

"I'm going to ask you one last time," Gibbs said, moving back around the table toward Austin. "Did you kill Kalama Kane?"

"And I'm going to repeat my answer... again. No! I did not kill my cousin. I had no reason to kill her."

When Gibbs and Tyrone started grilling Austin about his collection of medieval weapons, Talia wanted to scream.

Hadn't they already asked him those questions? She knew the process of interrogating a perp, but why were they asking him the same thing?

What bothered her was that Austin hadn't trusted her enough to tell her about his relationship with Kalama. Why? What could be embarrassing about a wayward cousin?

Kurt moved beside her and nudged her with his elbow. "We need to talk," he whispered.

"No, we don't." She didn't take her eyes off the men in the other room.

"I've been your partner for a year, and you're not going to give me a chance to explain?"

Anger rose higher inside of her, making her head pound harder. Yet, at the same time, her heart was shattering slowly, the more lies she heard from Austin, and definitely Kurt. She didn't know whether to yell or cry.

She turned and glared at Kurt. "Why would you want to explain? I'm not going to believe you." She shook her head, not caring if the sergeant overheard. "You know, it hurts," she placed her fist to her heart, "when someone you thought was a friend lies to you, but when someone you've known for so long, who is with you practically every day for a year, outright lies to your face, that's when the world tumbles and crashes all around. I'm sorry, Kurt, but I can't let you explain." She took a deep breath. "You aren't the person that I thought you were."

She pushed past him and darted out of the room, running down the hall. She couldn't get away from here fast enough, now.

NINETEEN

For three days, Talia couldn't bring herself to leave her apartment. She told Sergeant Feakes, she needed personal leave. Remarkably enough, he granted it to her. Now she wished Kurt would leave her alone. He came to see her several times, but she texted him to go away. He tried calling, tried texting, but she wouldn't respond. The fact that he'd withheld that tidbit about Austin and Kurt being stepbrothers was just too much for her to handle.

And then there was Austin… Although he hadn't told her the truth about being a billionaire, that didn't hurt as much as him withholding his relationship to Kalama, which was a very important part of their investigation. Why hadn't he told her? She knew why. Because it made him look guilty, especially after Kalama was killed.

Kurt had texted her to let her know that because of Austin's solid alibi, they had released him. Obviously, his ancient artifact had been used as the murder weapon, but according to the members of his board that were interviewed, Austin had been with them around the time of day when Kalama was murdered. And because of that, it appeared as though Austin might have been set up.

Talia really didn't know how to feel, anymore. She'd never cried so much in her life as she'd done these past three days. And all because of a man… two men, to be precise. Both men could have been the Prince Charming she'd been waiting for all of her twenty-five years. But in one night, she discovered that Prince Charming was a liar.

Frowning, she shook her head. Talk about ruining someone's life… and this one just happened to be a doozy. Not only had it ruined her trust with both men, but now she'd thought about putting in for a transfer. She wouldn't be able to work with Kurt Hamill after this.

The buzzing of her phone brought her out of her thoughts. Before answering, she checked the caller ID. It was her brother, Rongo. Wiping the tears from her eyes, she cleared her throat. "Hello." Inwardly, she grimaced. She still sounded like a frog with laryngitis.

"Talia? Is that you?"

"Yes."

"Are you sick?"

She sighed. Only sick in her heart. "No."

"Are you still coming to the family dinner tonight? Dad wanted me to call you and remind you that you can't miss out on this one."

She groaned. She had forgotten about it. Hopefully, she'd be able to get rid of her puffy eyes by tonight. "Yes, I'm coming."

"Great. Dad will be happy to hear. Do you want me to pick you up?"

Out of her three brothers, she was closer to Rongo since he was only two years older than her. Her other brothers wouldn't have even thought of picking her up. She smiled. "Sure. Sounds fun."

"Okay, I'll see you at six-forty-five tonight."

"Okay, bye."

She glanced at the clock on the DVD player. It was only ten o'clock in the morning? What was she going to do to pass the time? She couldn't get a good night's rest, because every time she closed her eyes, Austin's face was there. He wouldn't leave her memory. She'd recalled every moment they were together, and every word.

Why was his door opened that first day?

Curling on the couch, she hugged the large pillow. This was where she and Austin had cuddled and had a make-out session.

Had someone broken into his suite that morning?

She shook her head, trying to stop herself from thinking. She wasn't on the case anymore. Feakes took her and Kurt off immediately after learning how close she'd become with Austin, and especially because of Kurt's relationship with the suspect.

Austin hadn't been surprised that she had entered his suite...

"Augh!" She took the pillow and placed it over her head. Perhaps she needed a shrink. She couldn't get these voices out of her head. From now on, she didn't want anything to do with Kalama Kane's case.

The killer had returned the murder weapon to Austin's house to make him look guilty.

Slowly, she lowered the pillow and stared at the ceiling. Her mind started working the way it did when she was a police detective, and suddenly, she had left her own pity party. Somebody had set Austin up that knew how to get in and out of his penthouse suite. But who?

She put aside her dislike for him, and the fact that he broke her heart, because now she was in detective mode. Why hadn't she thought of this before? The reason Austin's door was open that first day was because someone else had been in there to return the weapon. Austin hadn't known why his door was opened, either. The doorknob hadn't appeared as if someone forced the door open. Nothing in his penthouse suite appeared to have been taken, so it wasn't a robbery.

Energy shot through her, and she jumped up to a sitting position. Whoever had returned the weapon must have a key. Could it be someone who worked in the hotel? For some reason, she didn't think so. Was it his maid? Then again, the ancient artifact was heavy, so she doubted the maid would be able to carry it. Whoever carried it must have been spotted by someone...

Security cameras!

Talia grabbed her cell and started to punch in Kurt's number, but then stalled. He wanted to see his stepbrother put behind bars. Even if the proof smacked him in the face, he wouldn't believe it. No, she had to be the one to solve this puzzle. She would be the one who would find the real killer.

She hurried into the bathroom to check her appearance in the mirror. *Ugh!* She stuck out her tongue. Considering she hadn't showered for two days – which meant she hadn't washed her hair – was it any wonder she looked so terrible?

Without another thought, she turned on the shower, shucked her clothes, and quickly washed herself. A half hour later, she was out the door and on her way to see Austin. She'd pulled her hair back in a ponytail, and didn't even bother to wear makeup. She wasn't going to see Austin to impress him. For once since meeting him, she was going to do her job and act like a professional detective and not a love-struck schoolgirl.

When she arrived at the hotel, it surprised her that she didn't have that giddy feeling that made her palms sweat and her heartbeat hammer like an out-of-control cheetah on steroids. Had her feelings for him disappeared so quickly? She hoped so. Being hung up on him would certainly put a damper on her life if she decided to start dating again.

She didn't know if he'd be home, but she had to take the chance that he would. On the elevator ride up to the penthouse suite, she rehearsed the words she'd say. No matter what, she couldn't allow him to sweet-talk her or charm her the way he'd done before.

When the elevator reached the floor and the door opened, right away she heard voices. As she cautiously stepped out into the hallway, she noticed a man talking with Austin. From what she could see, it appeared as if the man was just leaving.

Austin's gaze met hers, and he stopped talking. The expression on his face was unreadable, but she did notice he wasn't smiling as he'd been doing a moment ago.

The man glanced at her, and then muttered to Austin, "I'll see ya later." With his head down, he hurried past Talia and entered the elevator. She really only got a glimpse of him as he rushed by her, mainly because she couldn't stop looking at Austin. He wore a gray suit with a lavender shirt – minus the tie. He stood still as she walked toward him, and for some odd reason, her heart decided to pick up rhythm this time. Dang! Why couldn't she stay in control for once?

Something in the back of her head tugged at a memory. In an instant, the face of the man who'd been visiting with Austin flashed through her head, meeting with another memory of the same face. Heavenly Island Café! That's where she'd seen him… and he'd been with a blonde bombshell… the same woman who was the ditzy receptionist at Isabella's Escort Service.

Gasping, she stopped and swung around toward the elevator. The doors were closed, and the machine was already taking the man downstairs. She snapped around back to Austin and pointed toward the elevator. "Who was that man?"

"You don't know?"

"I've never met him, but I've seen him once before. Who is he?"

"That's my friend, Ariki."

Finally, puzzle pieces started fitting together. Excitement shot through her, the same way it had always done when she was about ready to solve a crime. "Austin, forgive me for coming without letting you know first, but… I think I might have just found the man who is trying to make you look like a killer."

His forehead creased, and then seconds later, his eyes widened. His gaze moved toward the elevator.

"Ariki? You think my friend set me up?"

"I know it sounds strange, but…" She sighed deeply and shifted her feet. "Austin, tell me something. Have you ever given your penthouse key to anyone?"

"No."

"Not even Ariki?"

"No. The only other person who has my key is my maid."

Talia paused in thought, still trying to fit all the pieces together. "Tell me, Austin, how did you meet your maid?"

"She's friends with—" His voice trailed off as color seeped from his face.

"With Ariki?" Talia finished for him.

He nodded. "But Ariki has no reason to want to set me up. He didn't even know Kalama that well." Austin turned back into his suite and walked to the liquor bar. He quickly grabbed a glass and the bottle of bourbon. "Do you want a drink?"

"No, I don't drink."

He threw her a scowl over his shoulder. "Those few times I poured you a glass, you didn't drink it?"

She shook her head.

He rolled his eyes and turned back to pouring his drink. "And yet you accuse *me* of lying to you," he muttered before tossing back the drink and swallowing hard.

How rude! And yet, he was accurate. Apparently, they'd both been hiding things from each other.

He cleared his throat. "Where did you see Ariki before?"

"Kurt and I discovered that Kalama had breakfast with someone at Heavenly Island Café the morning before she was killed. We'd gone there to ask questions. I noticed a man and woman seated, but it was the way the man kept trying to keep his face hidden from me that made me curious. When he and his woman friend left, they both looked like they didn't want us looking at them. And," she stepped closer to him, "you'll never guess where I just remember seeing the woman."

He shrugged. "Where?"

"She was the receptionist at Isabella's Escort Service." She paused, letting the information sink in his head a little. "Coincidence? I don't think so."

He huffed and set his glass upon the counter, then started pacing in front of her. "But that still doesn't make sense to me. Why would a friend I've known since I bought my first hotel, want to set me up? We've been best friends for several years. He's like the brother I never had."

"Austin? What is Ariki's last name?"

He paused in his pacing to look at her. "Martin. Why?"

Little by little, everything was fitting together. But what was Ariki's motive? She took slow steps toward Austin, and stopped when she reached him. She touched his arm. "The owner of Isabella's Escort Service is Mr. Martin. The ditzy blonde receptionist told us that when Kurt and I went there to ask questions. We could never find Mr. Martin. But I'd studied some pictures on the wall of that office, and the man who was in those pictures of the outdoors, was none other than your friend, Ariki." She took a deep breath and released it. "Did you know your friend owned a call girl business?"

"No," Austin said softly.

"That's how he met Kalama. And that's how he was able to find girls for you so easily to go out with."

"But..." He shook his head again. "I never once paid for his girls. Why would he do that if he owned the business?"

"Maybe he was trying to get you interested in a different way. Maybe he eventually wanted you to be one of their main clients."

Austin raked his fingers through his hair. "I wish I knew what his purpose was, especially if he took my weapon and killed Kalama with it. But we can't be sure, can we?"

"Actually, we can. Whoever took your weapon would have had to return it. Right?"

He nodded.

"Then I'm sure they'll be on your security cameras."

His eyes widened, and it was as if relief spread across his expression. "Yes, we could have caught it on the security footage."

She shrugged. "Well, what are we waiting for? Unless... do I need to obtain a warrant for you to release it to me?

"Of course not. Let's go look at it now."

He led them out of the suite and into the elevators. She kept her eyes on the electronic board that displayed what floor they were passing. Excitement bubbled inside of her, anticipating the thrill of finally solving this case.

Out of the corner of her eye, she could see Austin staring at her. Suddenly, her nervous stomach turned into something else, and the excitement flowing through her grew warm. *Not again!* Why couldn't she ignore these feelings she'd had for him? Why? Because she probably still had them.

"Talia, I need to apologize for not telling you the truth about Kalama."

Closing her eyes, she didn't like the way his pleading voice tugged on her heart. "No, you don't."

"Well, you'll have to listen to me, anyway. We're in an elevator, so you have no choice."

She looked back at the electronic display, thankful they were almost to the bottom level. "Only for a few more seconds."

He reached over and pushed the red emergency button on the panel. Immediately, the elevator stopped. The sudden movement from the contraption made her stumble and she fell against him. His strong arms tightened around her.

Heat consumed her, stronger than it had done before. And looking into his smoldering green eyes was her undoing. Little by little, her heart began to mend, even though she fought it from happening.

"Please, Talia, listen to me. I need to apologize and get this heavy restriction of guilt off my chest."

And speaking of chests… Her hands splayed upon his muscular frame, and just as before, she loved feeling his erratic heartbeat beneath her palms.

"At first, the reason I didn't tell you the truth about Kalama was because I was embarrassed that my cousin would go into that profession. You had once mentioned I had a kind and giving heart. Well, my kind and giving heart wanted to help her. No woman should have to lower themselves to do such a despicable thing. That's why I'd paid the escort service to let her go. When she returned to me earlier this year and begged my help again, I struggled to say no, but she was family, and I couldn't turn down her request."

He paused, and his beautiful green eyes reflected the pain he must be experiencing. A lump of emotion clogged her throat.

"Remember our evening at the park? I had decided to tell you then, but you had to leave. Later that night when you dropped by, I was determined to tell you the truth."

"Why didn't you?" she asked softly.

"Because you had confessed your true identity as a police detective. After that, I was scared that if I told you the truth, you would suspect me of being guilty – and I wasn't. I know I should have been honest with you, but I've had my share of bad policemen in my life, and I worried that you might be one of them. I have yet to see a policeman treat me as though I'm not the criminal. Just because I'm wealthy, doesn't mean I'm a terrible person."

Regret for everything she had thought about him the past three days flushed through her. Tears stung in her eyes, but she was so tired of crying, she didn't want to shed any more tears. She knew Austin well enough to know that he was telling the truth now. His expression was easy to read this time.

"What about Kurt and your family connection with him?"

He shook his head. "Kurt never liked me. I tried to become friends with him, but after a while of him trying to get me into trouble every time I turned around, I gave up. He didn't come visit his father very often, but when he did, he always threw accusations at me. I still don't know what I ever did to earn his hatred. My mother, on the other hand, was a terrible stepmother to Kurt, for which I feel awful about. I can only guess that Kurt took out his frustrations on me since he couldn't take it out on my mother." He stroked her hair as his gaze gently caressed her face. "Don't hate Kurt. I don't blame him. I'm sure his mother had said some terrible things about me and my mother. Kurt was only defending his mother, I'm sure of it."

Her heart finished thawing. In fact, it started melting again. Austin really did have a kind heart, just as she'd suspected. He should have more reason to hate Kurt than she did, and yet, Austin felt the need to forgive her partner. How could she not forgive Austin, especially now that she had a change of heart?

"And, what about that last thing that you withheld from me?" she asked.

"That I'm a billionaire?"

She nodded.

He shrugged. "I was treated differently growing up because my mother was rich. Most of the women I dated only went out with me because I bought them gifts. When I moved to Honolulu and was buying up resorts and hotels, I didn't want anyone to know exactly how much money I had. It was bad enough that they knew I was wealthy. But…" He shook his head. "I don't want people to like me for my money. I want them to like me for myself, and when I met you, that's what I wanted to happen. I didn't want you to look at me with dollar-signs in your eyes. I wanted you to look at me as though I was a real man… and interesting man who made you laugh." He stroked her cheek. "When I'd offered you the job and the opportunity to live in the penthouse suite, and you turned it down, I really felt I'd finally found the woman who liked *me* and not my money."

Blinking rapidly, she fought back the tears building behind her eyes. She was determined not to cry. "Thanks for explaining that to me. Now I feel rotten because I'd judged you so harshly."

He shook his head. "I should have trusted you sooner. I didn't know Kurt was your partner until that evening when you confessed everything to me. It was such a shock to me, and I didn't know who to trust. I should have gone with my heart. After all," he cupped her chin, "you had believed in my innocence when the other detectives hadn't. That means the world to me." He released a sigh. "Is there any way you can find it in your heart to forgive me?"

She laughed uncomfortably. "You probably think I'm a complete idiot now."

"Actually, I think you're the most amazing woman I've ever met."

Oh, why did he have to say that? The tears she tried to hold back came forth as though a dam had opened. "No, you are the amazing person, Austin Reeder," she said in a cracked voice.

He bent his head and captured her mouth with his eager lips. This time when the hot electric bursts of flame shot through her, it consumed her whole body. Every inch of her tingled with excitement, and although the kiss wasn't urgent as she'd experienced with him before, it was such a tender moment, one she never wanted to end.

Suddenly, there was a beeping noise coming from the control panel on the elevator, and then crackling in the speaker. "This is the hotel security. Is there a problem in the elevator?"

Both Talia and Austin broke apart laughing. He pushed another button. "Sorry, Rod. This is Austin Reeder. Everything is fine here."

"Oh, sorry to disturb you, Mr. Reeder."

As soon as the crackling sound disappeared, they both laughed harder. She playfully slapped his shoulder. "Austin Reeder? Have you done things on this elevator that are forbidden?" She wagged her eyebrows.

He gathered her back in his arms. "Not yet, I haven't. But there's always a first time for everything."

TWENTY

Austin kept his arm around Talia's waist as they sat side-by-side and watched the video surveillance from the security footage. His lips still tingled from her sultry kisses in the elevator, but with her standing next to him, the reassurance that everything would work out filled him, and made him feel calm.

Talia instructed the security guard on what day and time frame to look at. The hotel had a security camera at every entry door – four of them – and every hallway, but since they knew the killer would be returning the weapon to his room, that saved them from watching several recordings.

It was hard for him to watch the monitor screen instead of the beautiful woman next to him. She wasn't dressed fancy. But she still looked adorable in her gray T-shirt and faded jeans that fit nicely to her hips. She'd pulled her hair back into a ponytail, but he was getting used to that quickly. There was something different about her face, too. He didn't see that much make-up, but because she was a naturally gorgeous woman, it really didn't matter. He wasn't used to seeing her wearing her shoulder holster with the gun tucked inside, and her badge clipped to her pocket, however, he thought it made her more adorable... if that was possible.

In such a short time, Talia had become very dear to his heart. He couldn't imagine his life without her in it. Was it possible he'd fallen in love so quickly?

"We're looking for a person carrying something long and bulky," she told the security guard.

Austin forced himself to watch the monitor. He hoped it wasn't Ariki, and yet... he didn't know who else out of all of his friends knew that Austin was a collector of ancient weapons. If it was his friend, Ariki, Austin just wanted to know *why* he'd set him up.

"Pause it," Talia said in a raised voice.

Austin snapped out of his thoughts again and concentrated on the monitor. A man wearing a black hooded jacket had entered through the front doors, carrying an oblong box. His ancient weapon would definitely fit in that. Holding his breath, he leaned closer as he tried to see if the person looked familiar.

"Keep playing it, but go slowly," he instructed the security guard.

"He's carrying what appears like a flower box," Talia said. "Would the weapon fit in something like that?"

"It would."

The security guard, Rod, played the recording slower. Austin watched as the man walked up to the front desk. The hotel clerk chatted with the man for a few minutes. She pointed at the box. The man said something, and she laughed. Then the man moved toward the elevator. Why couldn't Austin see the person's face? He still didn't think this was Ariki.

"The desk clerk knows who that is." Talia tapped her finger on the monitor.

Austin moved his attention to her. "How can you tell?"

"I can read body language really well." She met his stare. "Did you notice the way the clerk smiled and batted her eyelashes at him? She also flipped a lock of hair over her shoulder. She wagged her fingers at him as he left. That tells me she's familiar with this man, and…" she placed her hand on his, "that also tells me this man comes to the hotel frequently."

He frowned. If this wasn't Ariki, then it was someone else close to him. He looked at Rod. "Let's see the recording for the hallway in front of the penthouse. And play it slow."

"Yes, Mr. Reeder." The guard quickly switched a few screens, and then pulled up the footage.

Austin studied the monitor again. The elevator doors opened and the man stepped out of the elevator, keeping his head lowered so it was impossible to see the man's face. When he reached Austin's door, he took out a key and slipped it in the keyhole. Immediately, something on the man's hand caught his attention. "Stop it!"

"What do you see?" Talia asked.

"Rod, zoom in closer."

"Yes, Mr. Reeder."

As the picture grew larger, Austin recognized the man's hand. Ariki also had a tattoo of an eagle on his right hand. Groaning, Austin covered his face with his hands.

"You know who it is, don't you?" Talia touched his shoulder. "Is it Ariki?"

He nodded his answer. "Rod, Detective Russell needs these tapes ASAP."

"Yes, sir. I'll get them ready for her right now."

Austin took Talia's hand and walked out of the security guard's station. She cuddled against his arm, rubbing the palm of her hand up and down his limb.

"Are you going to be all right?" she asked in a soft voice.

"Eventually. I just want answers. I still can't understand why Ariki would do all of this."

"We'll get answers, I promise."

Her sweet smile lightened his heart. He stopped their progress toward the lobby, and pulled her into his arms. "I trust you. You've not failed me yet."

"And I won't, not ever again."

Gazing into her amazing rusty colored eyes, he stroked her cheek. "Talia? Is it too soon to tell you I love you?"

She gasped and her mouth fell open. Shock was a mild description for her expression right now. Utterly stunned was more like it.

"You… you… you…" She licked her lips.

"Yes. You heard me correctly. I'm in love with you, Talia."

She bit her bottom lip as her eyes watered. "Oh, Austin. I can't believe you said it first. Usually I'm the one who says things like that first."

He arched an eyebrow. "You've told men you love them before?"

She released an uncomfortable laugh. "Well, not really. But usually I'm the one who is all mushy in a relationship, and the man has never returned my feelings."

"So what do you think?" Using the pad of his thumb, he stroked her bottom lip. "Do you think you love me, too?"

"Oh, yes, Austin. I love you, too, but I thought it was too early to say anything."

He shrugged. "Why wait? Life is short. We might as well tell each other how we feel now. That way, we can start our relationship sooner."

Sighing, she laid her head on his chest. "That sounds Heavenly."

He kissed the top of her head. "Okay, no more mushy stuff until we catch the bad guy."

She laughed and looked into his eyes. "I agree."

They turned and walked toward the lobby. Talia reached into her pocket and pulled out her cell. "I should probably call Kurt... No, I'll call Sergeant Feakes to let him know what we've found."

"That's a great idea. The quicker we can show them what happened, the sooner they will leave me alone."

She frowned and looked at him. "I'm so sorry this has happened to you."

"Me, too. But let's end it now."

He moved his gaze from her and back on the lobby as the hallway merged with the grand room. One figure stood out in the semi-crowded room. *Ariki!* Anger flared through Austin, hotter than he'd ever experienced before. Betrayal was not a tasty pill to swallow.

"Ariki!" he shouted.

His so-called friend jerked his attention toward Austin. His eyes widened.

In a flash, Talia withdrew her gun and pointed it toward Ariki. "Stop where you are."

Ariki took off running, as did the blonde woman who had been standing next to him.

Talia cussed, and threw her cell at Austin. "Call 911. Tell them an officer needs assistance."

Before he could stop her, she dashed after Ariki.

Austin's hands shook, either from fear or anger, as he dialed the number. He couldn't just stand there waiting, so he ran after Talia.

"9-1-1. What is your emergency?"

"I'm at the Imperial Hawaiian Grand Hotel on Park Street, and we have an officer in pursuit of a... killer." Bile rose from his throat. "She needs assistance. Immediately!"

"Sir?" the operator said quickly. "Are you all right? You sound out of breath."

"Just get her some help. She's running after the killer... and I'm running after her."

"All right, sir. Stay on the line and I'll call for some help."

Stay on the line? He slipped the cell in the pocket of his suit coat, and ran with all of his might. He was certainly wearing the wrong shoes for such an activity.

He kept his focus on the woman darting in and out of people, yelling at Ariki and the blonde to stop. The people on the street screamed and jumped out of her way, thankfully. The faster Talia rushed toward Ariki, the more her black, silky ponytail flapped on her back. He kept his eyes on that since she was getting farther ahead.

Austin's sides burned, along with his lungs, but he wouldn't stop. Talia needed his help in some way. He wouldn't abandon her.

When she turned and headed west, he could picture her location. This was an alleyway. Ariki wouldn't be able to escape. Thankfully, Talia had her gun. She wouldn't let them get away.

Sweat poured down Austin's face, and his muscles screamed with exertion, but he kept pushing onward. He quickly lifted the cell to his ear. The operator was still trying to get him to answer her. "Officer Russell turned down an alleyway between the Huntsman building, and the Tiki Shop, going west."

It hurt to talk. Hurt to breathe. He mustn't stop.

Through the air, he heard a gunshot. His heart dropped, and he muttered a quick prayer. Then another gunshot exploded through the air. *Please, Talia... be all right.*

He finally made it to the alley, and he turned, slowing down his steps. Up ahead, near a dumpster, Talia lay on the ground. Blood coated her gray T-shirt below her left breast. Her gun was on the pavement, out of reach. Sprawled on the ground next to her was the blonde woman, unconscious. But no blood stained her. Standing over Talia was Ariki.

With a gun!

Austin's mind scrambled. Ariki didn't know he was here, yet. If Austin could sneak up on him, maybe he could grab the man from behind and disarm him.

Taking careful steps, he moved toward Ariki.

"If you hadn't stuck your nose into my business, I wouldn't have to kill you," Ariki was telling Talia.

Color was disappearing from her face quickly. Austin prayed again that she wouldn't die.

"Why… why are you doing this?" Talia gasped for air as she clutched her side. Blood colored her fingers and trickled down her arms. "Why would you set up your best friend for murder?"

"You don't understand," Ariki yelled. "This was all Kalama's fault. If she had just been doing her job to begin with, none of this would have happened."

"Her job as a call girl? But Kalama was Austin's cousin."

"I know that," Ariki snapped. "Kalama was supposed to find something about Austin so we could blackmail him, just as we've been blackmailing the other wealthy and powerful men. But no! Austin is too pure, too sweet." Ariki's voice turned sarcastic. "That man's a freakin' fairy-tale, I swear!"

Austin bunched his hands, keeping them by his side. Every word from Ariki's mouth was ripping him apart.

"Is that why you killed Kalama?" Talia asked.

Ariki gave an evil laugh. "Can you believe it? She was trying to turn the tables on us, and blackmail us. Her own employer!"

"Is that…" Talia took a ragged breath. "Is that why your blonde friend poisoned her?"

"Yes, but when that didn't work, I stepped in and whacked Kalama over the head with Austin's weapon."

Austin was almost upon Ariki. He thanked the Almighty for not allowing Ariki to hear Austin.

Talia nodded. "I must hand it to you. That was a clever plan. Your friend would have never known."

"But now *you* know," he snapped, "and after I finish killing you, I have to kill Austin."

"What about the security guard?" she asked. "He knows, too."

Ariki spit out more cuss words. "Fine. I'll kill him after Austin. But first," he raised his hand and pointed the gun at her head, "I'm going to make sure you are out of the picture for good."

Suddenly, Austin recalled his training in college when he'd taken kickboxing lessons. Although he hadn't tried this for years, this was the only way to take Ariki down. He'd once been the best at a back-spin kick. He hoped he hadn't forgotten.

Pivot on the right leg. Kick with left leg. Whip head around toward target.

Focus... Focus...

Austin jumped into action, putting all of his energy into it. His leg connected with the back of Ariki's legs. The man cried out in pain and crumbled to the ground. The gun fell from his grasp. Austin regained his balance and kicked the gun farther away. Talia rolled just enough to pick up her gun. She pointed it at Ariki.

In the distance, sirens wailed through the streets. Austin wanted to sigh with relief, but Talia was still shot and bleeding profusely. He dropped to his knees beside her, yanking off his suit jacket. He wadded it into a ball and pressed it against her side.

Weakly, she smiled at him. "I'm glad you arrived when you had, or I'd be—"

"Shhh..." He placed a finger to her lips. "Don't talk. Save your energy. Help is on the way."

Her arm shook, lowering the gun. He took it from her and aimed it at Ariki. The man was still rolling on the ground in agony. At least Austin knew why Ariki had done all of this. He hoped his former friend got the death penalty. Then again, death was too good for him. He deserved to be tortured for the rest of his days.

Gently, Austin wrapped an arm around Talia. "You're going to be all right." Worry escalated as the color from her face disappeared, and her body grew weaker.

"Austin… I love you. I'm sorry we couldn't… be together."

"No!" he said in a commanding tone. "You are not going to die. Do you hear me? You will live through this, and I will take care of you." His throat clogged with emotion, and he swallowed hard. "Talia, look at me. My strength will give you strength. I can't lose you. I won't be able to live without you in my life. So if you give up, you'll be ending my life, as well. Do you want that on your conscience?"

Her weak gaze met his and she smiled faintly. "When did… you take up… kickboxing?"

He chuckled lightly. "In college. Do you know how to do it, too?"

"Yes."

"Then instead of arm wrestling, let's do a round of kickboxing."

Her smile stretched. "You're on."

TWENTY-ONE

Talia's pain level was lower than normal. Either that or she'd taken a bullet somewhere she wasn't used to hurting. She'd taken bullets before, but none of them had made her nearly bleed to death like this one had.

As she lay in the hospital bed with tubes running through her arms, in addition to the IV, she watched the nurse shoot another dose of pain medication from the syringe to her tubing. Soon, she'd feel fine.

The operation had been successful, thank goodness. But she had lost a lot of blood. The doctor had mentioned that she was very lucky. The bullet grazed off her rib and barely missed piercing her kidney by half an inch. If the bullet would have punctured an organ, she certainly wouldn't be laying in this hospital bed, complaining of her pain. But now, she just had to worry about the discomfort from the stitches, and the bruised rib.

If it hadn't been for Austin's quick thinking, she would have been dead with a bullet through the head. He had thought of the best way to take Ariki down. If Austin would have jumped on him, there was the chance that Ariki would have pulled the trigger, anyway. But because Austin brought instant pain to the man's legs, that's what made him release the gun.

The cops and ambulance had shown up immediately. Her team wasn't too far behind. Not long after that, she had passed out, probably because of her low blood levels. When she'd awakened, the doctor assured her she would be fine. She had only wanted one thing at that moment. Austin. Thankfully, the hospital staff allowed him inside the recovery room.

When he first looked at her, tears had filled his eyes as he smiled. This amazing man was so incredibly loving and caring. How had she gotten to be so lucky?

Now, sitting in her hospital room, she wanted to see him again before the meds took over and made her silly and sleepy.

"Is Austin Reeder in the waiting room?" Talia asked.

"Do you mean that good-looking rich man who has been tipping all of your nurses one-hundred dollars?"

Talia laughed. "Yes, that sounds like something he'd do."

"He's still here. I don't think he's left the hospital since you arrived. And, if you can believe this," the woman leaned down closer as if to tell Talia a secret, "he even had one of his servants bring him a new change of clothes."

"That's definitely something he'd do." Talia nodded.

The nurse straightened and turned to place the empty syringe in the plastic container. "And your co-workers are waiting to talk to you, as well." The forty-year-old nurse wagged her eyebrows. "You definitely work with some good-looking men. And here I thought that happened only in the movies or on TV."

"Yes, I have to admit, I do work with some very handsome men."

"Would you like them to come in? This medication will make you tired very shortly."

"I know." Talia licked her dry lips. "Let them in. Let all of them in."

"Of course."

"And hurry," Talia added. "Before I fall asleep."

Once the nurse left, Talia used the remote to adjust her bed to help sit her up a little more. She arranged the blankets around her legs and waist. She really couldn't reach her hands to the top of her hair to make sure she didn't appear like a raving lunatic with hair flying all over the place, so hopefully she didn't look that way, or her visitors would have the decency not to mention it.

Austin was the first one to come in. His smile was wide, and his eyes glimmered with love. Her heart melted, again. But now, she actually enjoyed that feeling.

"You're looking better." He kissed her briefly on the lips.

"I'm sure. White looks better on me than blood red."

"In this case, it does." He stroked her fingers, lovingly. "I just realized that your family doesn't know. Would you like me to call them for you?"

Inwardly, she groaned, and switched her gaze to the clock on the wall. Nine thirty-five. "I'm sure they've been trying to reach me since we were to have a family dinner at seven o'clock this evening."

"Let me call them and explain." He reached in his pocket for his cell.

"No, I will. They don't know who you are yet."

A movement from the doorway caused her to shift her gaze. Kurt walked in first, followed by Sergeant Feakes, and then Gibbs and Tyrone. Kurt held flowers for her.

"Hey," she said, meeting Kurt's sorrowful gaze. Her heart didn't flip like it used to when looking upon his gorgeous face. And now it made her happy knowing she didn't hate him anymore.

"For a speedy recovery," Kurt said, holding up the vase of flowers.

"Mahalo, Kurt. They're lovely."

He set them by the window, before moving to her and kissing her forehead. "How are you?"

"I'm going to be fine. The nurse just gave me a shot of painkillers."

He chuckled. "She told us not to stay long."

Austin moved aside as each one came over to her and kissed her forehead. She thanked each one, individually.

"So," she said, "did you catch the killer?"

Sergeant Feakes shook his head. "No, you did." He arched an eyebrow, critically. "Remind me later to reprimand you for going after the killer even when I had taken you off the case."

"Yeah, well… you know me. Headstrong. Besides, I couldn't let him get away. And," she pointed to Austin, "I told him to call for backup."

"He did," Kurt said, giving Austin a look of gratitude. "If not for you, we would have lost her." His voice cracked.

"I did all I could," Austin answered with a smile.

Talia rested her head back on the pillow as her mind grew foggier by the second. "Oh, you should have seen him. He was incredible. I thought he was Jackie Chan popping out of nowhere from one of his action movies, to take down the bad guy." She giggled as her mind played back the scene with Austin.

His face turned red. He lowered his head and bit back a grin as her coworkers laughed.

"Sounds like Talia is drifting off to la-la-land," Gibbs mentioned.

"What happened?" Feakes asked with a touch of humor in his voice.

Talia was shocked. The man who never smiled, actually was doing it now. Good grief… he did have teeth, and they were real!

"Oh, you should have seen it," Talia began excitedly. "He did a-ha," she tried to position her hands correctly as if she was ready to do a Karate chop, "and a hi-yah, and… he kicked him down to the ground, sir. Ariki rolled around in pain, screaming like a girl." She giggled even more.

"Talia?" Austin asked, stepping closer and laying his hand on her shoulder. "What happened with the ditzy blonde? When I arrived, she was already out cold."

"Well," she paused, waiting for the wave of dizziness in her head to pass, "when I ran into the alleyway, blondie jumped on me, which knocked my G42 out of my hand. We wrestled for a bit, but I had her down, and I was able to knock her unconscious with one blow of my fist. That's when Ariki shot me from behind." She gently touched her bandaged middle.

"So, Reeder is our hero?" Kurt walked up to Austin and patted his shoulder. "We have you to thank for saving our Talia's life."

Austin offered Kurt a kind smile. "I acted on instinct. I knew I couldn't let her die." He looked at Talia and took her fingers gently in his hand. "I couldn't lose the woman I'd fallen madly in love with."

"I'm glad." She sighed as her eyes slowly closed. "Because I didn't want to lose the man I'd fallen madly in love with, either."

* * * *

Every other step Talia took, she winced. She was on her way to making a full recovery, but unfortunately, her father's wedding came upon her and she knew she had to attend. Although she'd missed the family dinner, they had all dropped by to visit with her while she was in the hospital. Some days, Patricia came by herself. It was a little awkward at first for Talia, but soon she saw what her father had seen in this woman. True, she wasn't Talia's mother because nobody could fill those shoes, but Patricia was well suited for her father. And they were happy. That's all that mattered.

"My sweet lady," Austin said as he helped her walk while keeping his arm around her waist, staying clear of her wound, "I told you we should have gotten you a wheelchair."

"I don't need a wheelchair."

Once inside the chapel, she paused, putting her weight against him. She nodded to guests attending the wedding, some she remembered from her childhood. Glancing up at Austin, she grinned. "You're better than a wall."

"What?" His mouth quirked.

"What I meant was, I'd rather have you hold me up than the wall. You're more comfortable."

He kissed her forehead. "I'm always comfortable in your arms, too."

Could she love and adore this man any more than she already did? Not only had he saved her life, but since she was released from the hospital, he played her nursemaid twenty-four, seven. He either put his meetings on hold, or he conducted them over his cell or computer, only so he could stay and care for her.

"Have I told you lately that I love you?" she whispered.

He nodded. "This morning as I helped you dress." His gaze swept over her dress. Desire lit his eyes. "And, I might say, I did a pretty good job."

She glanced down at the brand new, ankle-length dress Austin had purchased for her just for her father's wedding. The silky, hot-pink sensation fit her body perfectly, and actually made her look as if she had a curvy figure. Apparently, he'd thought so too, because she caught him drooling several times.

Instead of pulling her hair back into a ponytail, she kept it long and wavy, just the way Austin liked it. He couldn't stop running his fingers through her locks. But she didn't mind at all. She enjoyed watching the pleasure on his face when he did small, intimate, things like this.

He looked mighty fine, as well, wearing a black, cashmere, single-breasted Armani suit with a white shirt and hot pink tie to match her dress. She wasn't sure she liked the women ogling him with their stares, but Talia supposed that if she had such a handsome man for a boyfriend, she'd just have to get used to other women staring with stars in their eyes.

After all, that's how she had looked when she first saw him.

"I'm ready now." She tapped him on the chest. "Let's go into the chapel and find a seat, but I don't want to sit up front."

"Why not?"

"In case I have to go to the bathroom or something. I'll need you to help me walk."

He laughed. "Your wish is my command, my wonderful woman."

Being so very tender with her, he walked them inside and found a place near the back. Once they were seated, she leaned against him, resting her head on his arm. She noticed her brothers right away. The oldest, Danno, was sitting with his pregnant wife who was ready to deliver any day now. He had lighter brown hair, like their mother had, but he inherited his height from their father.

Sean, the second to the oldest, was getting his master's degree. He'd soon get his doctorate. He started out with lighter hair, but over the past few years, it grew darker. She figured he would have black hair like her, eventually.

Rongo was in college, too, but his interest was in law. He'd told her once he either wanted to be a police officer, or a lawyer. Maybe that was why they were closer because they shared the same passion for justice and fighting bad guys. They also shared the same color of eyes, and hair. Throughout their years, people had commented that they could have been twins.

When her brothers saw her, they waved, and she returned a small wave. She moved her attention to the decorations. Everything was so beautiful. Patricia had chosen green and tan for her colors. The bride and groom decided not to have bridesmaids or groomsmen, mainly because they'd both been married before. They wanted a simple ceremony, no more than fifty guests. Instead of a reception, they elected to have a dinner at a local restaurant, inviting only family and close friends.

If Talia had wanted a small wedding, that's what she would have done, too. But ever since she was a small girl, she'd always wanted a large wedding ceremony, with several bridesmaids and groomsmen, a flower girl, and a ring bearer. Her colors would be deep purple and silver. She wanted a fairy-tale gown, but not so overly decorated that the guests couldn't see the bride.

In all of her dreams, she hadn't been able to see the groom's face. But she knew he had short, dark brown hair. She also knew he'd have hypnotic green eyes, and a magnificent smile.

Tilting her head back, she looked at Austin. He was the perfect man. He loved her for herself, even if she didn't wear a lot of makeup. He didn't mind when she had her hair in a ponytail, either. Rarely had she worn dresses, and he was all right with that, too – although, he nearly devoured her when he saw her in this dress. Last, but not least, she hadn't told him I love you first, because he had confessed it. That meant he really did love her.

He looked at her. "Are you feeling all right? Are you in any pain?"

"No pain." She shook her head. "And I'm feeling wonderful. I have the best man in the world, and my heart is full of love. What can be better than that?"

He cupped her face and tenderly kissed her lips, briefly. "You make me so happy. I want this feeling to last forever."

"Me, too." She kissed him one more time before pulling back.

"So, what are we going to do about it?" He arched an eyebrow.

"What do you mean?" Her heartbeat quickened, wondering… hoping… anticipating what he was going to say next.

He chuckled. "Well, being here in this church, admiring all of the beautiful decorations, it's made me wonder what our wedding is going to be like."

Her heartbeat kicked into overdrive and she couldn't control the grin stretching wide across her face. "You, too, huh?"

"Yes."

"I didn't know men did that."

He laughed. "Some men do, especially when we've found the perfect woman."

"Well, I don't know." She cocked her head. "You haven't even proposed to me yet."

The laugh-lines in his forehead and around his eyes relaxed. "I'll have to fix that, won't I?"

"Only if you want."

"Oh, believe me, I want. But, it won't be today."

"Good." She cuddled by his side again. "Because I want you to surprise me."

"My dearest, Talia. Every day with you will be a wonderful surprise, and I look forward to more of them."

She wanted to kiss him again, but when the organ started playing the wedding march, she decided to be quiet and watch the ceremony.

Happiness burst inside her chest. This would be her in a few short months, and then she'd be with Austin Reeder, the love of her life, throughout all eternity.

What could be better than that… besides a few kids and a white picket fence?

THE END

ABOUT THE AUTHOR

Since Marie Higgins was a little girl playing Barbies with her sister, Stacey, she has loved the adventure of making up romantic stories. Marie was only eighteen years old when she wrote her first skit, which won an award for Funniest Skit. A little later in life, after she'd married and had children, Marie wrote Church roadshows that were judged as Funniest and Best Written. From there, she branched out to write full-length novels based on her dreams. (Yes, she says, her dreams really are that silly)

Marie has been married for several years to a wonderful man. Together, they have three loving daughters and several beautiful grandchildren. Marie works full time for the state of Utah, where she has lived her entire life. Marie plans to keep writing, because the characters in her head won't shut up. But her husband smiles and pretends this is normal.

Marie Higgins is a best-selling author of Christian and sweet romance novels; from refined bad-boy heroes who make your heart melt to the feisty heroines who somehow manage to love them regardless of their faults. She has over 60 heartwarming on-the-edge-of-your-seat stories, and broadened her readership by writing mystery/suspense, humor, time-travel, paranormal, along with her love for historical romances. Her readers have dubbed her "Queen of Tease", because of all her twists and unexpected endings.

Website – https://www.authormariehiggins.com
Facebook – http://www.facebook.com/marie.higgins.7543
Twitter – https://twitter.com/mariehigginsXOX
Pinterest - https://www.pinterest.com/mariehigginsxox/
Bookbub - https://www.bookbub.com/authors/marie-higgins
Phone reading apps - https://www.ficfun.com   AND
https://www.dreame.com AND https://www.radishfiction.com/

Made in the USA
Las Vegas, NV
27 October 2022

58235152R00092